CMD

Ty'n ôl i'r stoc
Withdrawn

Raintree is an imprint of Capstone Global Library Limited, a company incorporated in England
and Wales having its registered office at 264 Banbury Road, Oxford, OX2 7DY – Registered
company number: 6695582

www.raintree.co.uk
myorders@raintree.co.uk

Edited by Julie Gassman
Designed by Hilary Wacholz
Illustrated by Kirbi Fagan
Production by Tori Abraham
Printed and bound in China

ISBN 978-1-4747-3400-4 (paperback)
21 20 19 18 17
10 9 8 7 6 5 4 3 2 1

British Library Cataloguing in Publication Data
A full catalogue record for this book is available from
the British Library.

DARK WATERS

INTO THE STORM

A MERMAID'S JOURNEY

by JULIE GILBERT

illustrated by KIRBI FAGAN

raintree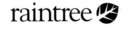

a Capstone company — publishers for children

My name is India Finch. People say it's a funny name. India is a country, and a finch is a kind of bird. A country and a bird. It's an odd name for someone who is a mermaid. Well, part mermaid.

Confused? Me too. I didn't know I was part-mermaid until this summer. I'm spending the summer with my grandpa on the coast of Cornwall. It's beautiful here. Lots of Cornish palm trees, harbours and beaches. And the ocean is amazing. The sea stretches forever and ever. The waves crash against the rocks.

The ocean makes me feel huge and small at the same time. It feels like home.

I was shocked when Grandpa told me he was part-mer. I thought he was joking. Turns out he wasn't. Grandpa's mother was a mermaid. He's part-mer, and so am I.

On the outside, I look like an ordinary girl. I have medium brown skin, dark brown eyes and crinkly dark hair. I get my stubborn chin from my mum and my crooked ears from my dad. I'm tall for my age, and my arms and legs are strong.

I look like an ordinary girl in the water too. When I'm in the ocean, I don't grow a tail or gills. But salt water activates my mer abilities. I can breathe water instead of air. I can also swim for miles and miles without getting tired. And I can use my hands to heal injuries and illnesses. I have extra powers because I'm female. All mermaids have powers, but none of the mermen do.

My mermaid friends have amazing powers too.

Nari can talk to sea creatures using her mind. She can communicate with fish and lobsters and seals.

She says the sea creatures make better friends than most of the mer.

Dana can make water thick. When she does, I feel as if I'm swimming in clear jelly. She likes to tease us sometimes. We'll be swimming along, and suddenly the water is too thick to move.

Lulu can move currents and make waves. She's really strong, just like her personality. I shouldn't have favourites, but I like Lulu the best. She's a fighter, like me. Or at least how I want to be.

The mer used to live all over the oceans. That's why so many cultures have stories about mermaids, even though people don't believe in mermaids. It's funny that humans don't know the mer are real. Humans are to blame for so many mer problems, after all.

Mer homes have always been protected by domes. The domes are like giant snow globes that make whatever is inside invisible. The dome forms naturally when the mer live in harmony with their surroundings. Once people started drilling for oil, laying cables and polluting oceans, mer homes were destroyed. The domes protecting the mer collapsed.

The mer started to die out. Fearing extinction, the remaining mer banded together and formed two tribes. Even though the tribes don't always get along, the mer are safer together than apart.

Almost three hundred mer live in two tribes in the deep underwater valleys called canyons off the coast of Cornwall. My mermaid friends are part of the Ice Canyon tribe. The other tribe is the Fire Canyon tribe. Neither tribe likes humans.

The Ice Canyon tribe wants to leave the humans alone. Live and let live, they say. The Fire Canyon mer are different. They want to attack humans and punish them.

Members from the different tribes aren't supposed to hang out with each other. This means I can't spend as much time with Evan as I'd like to. He's one of the Fire Canyon mer. He's also really smart – and cute. He seems to like me too.

I don't know how long I'll be able to hang out with Evan or any of my friends. Grandpa told me that when he was a young man, he had to choose between living on land or in the sea.

He had fallen in love with my grandmother. She was human. Because of her, Grandpa chose land. But he pledged that his children and grandchildren would always help the mer.

Unfortunately my dad wanted nothing to do with the mer. He used to swim with them when he was my age, but then something happened. Dad made a bad decision, and a mermaid died. I don't know the whole story and neither does Grandpa.

When he was old enough, Dad moved to the West Midlands. Grandpa said Dad wanted to keep me away from the ocean while I was growing up. As a kid, I never knew I was part-mer. But I think Dad wanted me to know. Right before I got on the train, Dad took me by the shoulders.

"Trust Grandpa," he said. "Whatever he says. No matter how crazy it sounds."

Then he hugged me tight and walked away.

I didn't know what Dad meant until I came to Cornwall and discovered my mer abilities. I still don't know if my mum knows. Even if Dad told her, I'm not sure she'd believe him.

The first time I talked with Dad on the phone, I asked him about the mer. I told him how shocked I was to learn the news. And that I wanted to know everything.

"We'll talk about it when you get home," was all he said.

I like being with the mer. They call me when they need my help by sending a seaweed wreath. Then I jump into the ocean to be with my friends.

Because I'm half-human, the dome makes it impossible for me to find the canyons on my own. The canyons are invisible to me until I'm inside the dome.

My human eyes can't see the dome, either, although it's supposed to be beautiful. My friends have to take me to and from the canyons where the mer live.

We have lots of wild adventures. Sometimes, though, I wonder if the mer only like me because of my powers. I'm the only one who has healing powers, after all. Would they even want me around if I couldn't help them?

I also wonder what my future holds. Will I have to make the same choice Grandpa did? Will I have to choose between my human side and my mermaid side? I'm not sure. I don't know which side I'd pick.

Maybe one day I'll know for sure.

CHAPTER 1

*P*link. *Plink. Plink.*

The noise wakes me up. I press my arm over my eyes and roll over. The sheets are sweaty, but I find a cool spot on my pillow. I try to get back to sleep.

I was in the middle of a great dream. I'd been winning the two-hundred-metre butterfly event at the Olympics. Everyone was cheering for me. My arms tore through the water. I felt free. I had almost touched the wall when–

Plink. Plink.

"Ugh, what's making that noise?" I groan.

The dream slides from my mind. For a second I think I'm at home in Birmingham. I struggle to remember what day it is. Am I going to be late for school? Why didn't Mum wake me up?

Then I smell salt water. That's right. I'm in Cornwall for the summer, staying with Grandpa. My parents are back home, doing couples therapy or something. They sent me away. They said it was for the best.

Was it? I'm not sure, but I suppose I'll find out at the end of the summer.

Being here isn't so bad. I like getting to know Grandpa. The ocean is amazing. I love to walk along the beach and watch the waves. And I spend my time helping my mermaid friends.

I open my eyes to the wallpapered walls of my room. The windows are open. Red polka-dot curtains float in the breeze. Rain hits the glass and splatters on the floor.

"Well, that explains the sound," I mutter, turning onto my back.

I get out of bed and close the windows. The rain has left puddles on the floor. I pull a beach towel from a shelf and drop it on the water. I mop up the puddles with my foot.

Yawning, I start brushing out my hair. I put on extra leave-in conditioner last night, so my hair is smooth and easy to comb.

After my hair falls in poofy curls around my shoulders, I get dressed and head to the kitchen. Grandpa is there, munching granola.

"Morning, Grandpa," I say, grabbing an apple.

"Would you like some toast?" he asks.

"Yes please," I say.

Grandpa puts two slices of wholegrain bread into the toaster. I kick my foot against the chair. Grandpa slurps his coffee.

"It's raining," I say.

"Yep," Grandpa replies. He's a man of few words. I don't mind. When I'm at home, I'm always chattering with someone. My mum, my dad, all of my friends. But here, I'm learning that I like silence too.

The toast pops up. I slide the warm pieces onto a plate and slather them with butter.

"Have we got any jam?" I ask.

"In the fridge," Grandpa says. He gestures with his coffee mug. That's all we say for awhile.

"Is it supposed to rain all day?" I ask, putting my empty plate in the sink.

"Sounds as if it should be letting up in a few minutes," Grandpa says. He nods at the small weather radio on the counter.

The radio is the most technological thing we have at the cottage. Grandpa doesn't have a TV, computer or tablet. Oh, and there's no mobile phone reception. If I want to send a text or check the Internet, I have to walk into town.

I may not mind the silence, but I really miss my phone.

"Weather's supposed to get worse," Grandpa adds.

"Oh?" I ask.

"Bad storm might be coming," he says.

I glance out of the window. The rain is stopping.

"Today?" I ask.

Grandpa actually laughs, a low, rusty sound. "Not today. But there's a hurricane they're watching in the Atlantic."

"Will it hit us here?" I ask.

"It might," Grandpa says. "They usually burn out before they reach Cornwall, but we'll probably get some heavy rain and wind."

I remember seeing pictures on TV of severe storms in Devon a few years ago. People's homes were flooded. "Do we need to prepare?" I ask. "Get sandbags? That kind of thing?"

Grandpa sips his coffee. "I doubt it. We'll keep an eye on it, though."

He stretches and reaches for his name tag on the counter. Grandpa works at the marine sanctuary in town.

"Don't want to be late for my shift," he says.

"Well, I'm off to the beach," I say.

"Are you sure?" Grandpa asks. He peeks out of the window. A fine mist is still falling.

"Um, yeah," I say, grabbing my beach bag. It's crammed with sun cream, towels and swimwear.

"Have they called you?" Grandpa asks. He puts his mug on the counter.

Grandpa is talking about my mermaid friends, Nari, Dana and Lulu. When the mer need my help, my friends send a seaweed wreath. Sometimes I think I've spent most of my summer waiting for my friends.

"That's what I'm going to find out," I say, slinging the bag over my shoulder. "So I might not be back for dinner."

Grandpa huffs.

"Is that a problem?" I ask. I know Grandpa doesn't like it when I'm gone for too long.

"Leave a note, at least," Grandpa says.

"Okay," I say, slipping on my sandals.

"Wait," Grandpa says.

"What is it?" I ask, pausing in the doorway.

"I just don't want you to feel bad," Grandpa says at last. "If they haven't called you."

"I won't," I say, but I know Grandpa has a point. I hate the empty feeling I get when my friends haven't called me.

I say goodbye to Grandpa and leave the cottage. The front door slams shut behind me.

The sky is grey, and a light mist coats my hair. It's hard to tell if the mist is rain or fog blowing in from the ocean.

I decide it's fog and keep walking towards the beach. I'd rather be outside than cooped up in the cottage. I've already read all of Grandpa's books, plus most of the books at the tiny public library.

When I get to the beach, it's empty. There's a lot of sand and rocks. On one end, there's a path leading to a small forest. The town is on the other side, but I can't see it from here.

I can't count the hours I've spent walking this beach, looking for a seaweed wreath from my mermaid friends.

Today, I'm in luck. I can see the wreath bobbing on the edge of the water. I race towards it, my feet sinking into the sand.

"Finally!" I say to the ocean.

I run to the cliffs that jut into the water. Dropping my bag behind a rock, I climb up. I check the beach behind me. Technically, no one is supposed to be on the cliffs. They overlook churning water. Even strong swimmers would get hurt or killed by the waves here.

Fortunately, my mer powers protect me. I have nothing to fear from the water.

When I reach the edge, I get into a crouch and swing my arms. I draw a breath of cool, salty air. The mist coats my cheek. Soon I'll be breathing salt water through my lungs.

I pause for a moment. I'm supposed to leave Grandpa a note.

"He'll be fine," I mutter. I don't want to go back to the cottage. I'm too eager to see my friends. I look over the water. I deepen my crouch. Then I jump.

CHAPTER 2

The ocean is cold. I feel as if I've jumped into an ice bath. My body needs a few minutes to adjust. The air leaves my body before the water can flow into my lungs. I hate how it feels, as if I'm going to drown. Salt water stings my eyes, and my arms and legs feel heavy.

Then, like magic, my mer powers take over. My eyes clear, my lungs expand. I feel as if I can fly through the water.

My mermaid friends hover in front of me. Lulu, with her dark hair and skin, her tail flapping back and forth. Dana and Nari, holding hands, Dana's red curls tangling with Nari's long black hair.

"Hi, everyone!" I yell with a grin on my face. I brace myself for the moment when they all rush and gather around me.

But the hugs don't come.

"What's going on?" I ask. I study their faces. Their mouths are tense, and their eyes are wide. "Why do you all look worried?"

Nari glides forward on her sapphire blue tail. She slides her arms around my shoulders and gives me a hug.

"We're glad you're here, India," she whispers into my hair.

"What's going on?" I ask. "Or should we wait until we get to Ice Canyon before you tell me?"

Lulu shakes her head. "We're not going to Ice Canyon. Not this time."

"Why not?" I ask. "What's happening? You guys are starting to freak me out."

Dana's face is pale, but she laughs. "Don't be freaked out," she says, squeezing my arm.

"But why do you all look so weird?" I ask.

Lulu sighs. "We all know how much you love Ice Canyon," she says. "We weren't sure how you would react."

"React to what?" I ask. I look at each of them. "You guys aren't making any sense."

Nari takes my hands. "India, you can't come to Ice Canyon," she says gently. "Not this time. Please don't be mad."

Oddly enough, I wasn't mad until now.

I jerk my hands free from Nari's grasp. "So you think I can't handle not going to the canyon?" I say. My voice is getting higher and higher. "You think I'm going to break down because I can't go? Well, you're wrong!"

My friends exchange glances. A part of me knows I'm proving their point by yelling. But a bigger part of me is too angry to care.

"Look, India—" Nari says.

"Look at what?" I demand, interrupting her. "Why did you even bother to summon me? Just to tell me I'm no longer welcome at the canyon?"

"Calm down, India," Lulu commands. She is always ready to take control of a situation. "Ani sent us. We summoned you because the mer need help. You're not banned from Ice Canyon."

"There's a big storm coming," Dana says.

"Yeah, Grandpa mentioned something about it this morning," I grumble. "But he said it would probably burn itself out."

"They usually do," Lulu says. "But this one looks different."

"The canyons are far below the surface of the water," I say. "Could a storm damage them?"

"Everything gets thrown off balance when there's a storm," Lulu says. "The worst storms can disrupt our powers. The waters get stirred up and make us weak."

"It could also wreck the dome protecting the canyons," Nari adds.

"Oh," I say. My anger deflates. I suppose it's fine I never left a note for Grandpa. I'll be going right back home. "I didn't know. Um, what do you need me to do?"

"We need you to keep track of the reports on land," Lulu says. "And then meet us and tell us what you find out."

"Can you help us?" Nari asks.

I think about Grandpa's radio. And the Lucky Lobster bar and cafe in town has TV. I can't track the storm on my phone, but I can get them information.

"Yes, I can do that," I say.

My friends look relieved.

"Good," Lulu says. "We'll meet you here in a few hours. You can tell us what's happening."

"Okay," I say, trying to ignore the feeling of disappointment. I would much rather be going to Ice Canyon with my friends. Instead I'll be stuck on land.

I think Nari notices my disappointment. "We can stay for a little bit, India. Do you want to swim around here with us?"

"I'd love to," I say.

"Great!" Nari says.

We all swim out into the ocean, away from the cliffs. A pod of dolphins greets us, nosing us with their long snouts. I pat one on the head.

Eventually the dolphins lose interest in us. They chirp at each other and swim away.

"How's Ice Canyon?" I ask at the same time Nari is asking, "How's your grandpa?"

"He's fine," I say.

"Everything's fine at home," Dana volunteers. "We've mainly been hanging out at the *Clemmons*."

"Oh," I say.

The *Clemmons* is an old steamer ship that sank a hundred years ago. It lies on its side halfway between Ice and Fire Canyon, where the mer live. A lot of the younger mer hang out at the ship. It's my favourite spot in the canyons, mainly because that's usually where I see Evan.

Evan.

My heart lurches. Evan's not my boyfriend or anything. But there's something between us. I shake my head, my curls bouncing in the water. I don't want to think about Evan, not when I'm already sad.

"How's your mum?" I ask Lulu.

"Ani's fine," she says. She blows a stream of water out of her mouth. "She's been talking to Storm a lot, trying to make sure the tribes don't fight."

Storm and Ani are the leaders of the two tribes that live in the canyons. Both tribes want to stay away from humans.

My friends are a part of the Ice Canyon tribe, which wants to ignore humans. Ice Canyon fights with the Fire Canyon mer, because the Fire Canyon mer want to attack humans. So far they've left humans alone, but there have been some close calls.

"What does Storm think about Ani's plans?" I ask. Storm is the leader of Fire Canyon. He doesn't like me much. I don't like him much either. Which makes things complicated, since Storm is Evan's dad.

"He says he agrees," Lulu says. "Who knows what he really thinks."

"I think Storm wants to prevent war between the tribes," Nari pipes up.

We all turn to look at her.

"What?" she asks. "I pay attention."

We all laugh, and it breaks the tension. Soon we are swimming lazy circles around each other.

"Storm and Ani are hosting another dinner," Lulu says. "Everyone's supposed to be there."

"When is it?" I ask.

"Tonight," Lulu replies.

My heart lurches again. If I was invited to the canyons, I'd be going to the dinner. And Evan would be there.

"I told Mum we didn't have to have a dinner this week," Lulu is saying. "Especially since the dance is only a few days away."

"Wait, what?" I ask.

Everyone stops swimming. I prop my hands on my hips and kick my feet to stay afloat. My friends all glance at each other. They look guilty.

"There's a dance?" I ask, my voice squeaky.

"Um," Lulu says.

"Um?" I repeat. "Is that all you have to say?"

Nari is clutching her hands. "We were going to tell you, India."

"Yeah, we were," Dana adds.

"It's just ... it's just no big deal," Lulu says, not meeting my eye.

"No big deal? Then why not tell me about it?" I ask.

"We didn't want you to feel left out," Dana says, swimming to my side. "Honest."

"Please don't be mad," Nari pleads. Her eyes are filled with tears.

I sigh. "So I suppose I'm not invited to this dance." I can't decide if I'm more mad or more sad.

"Lulu asked," Nari says.

"You did?" I ask, looking at Lulu.

She nods. "I went to my mum and begged her to let you come."

"And?" I ask.

"She said it was too dangerous," Lulu says.

"Dangerous how?" I ask.

"The dance is for both the Fire and Ice mer," Lulu explains. "It's supposed to bring the tribes together. Unite them. And having a human, even a part-mer human..." Lulu's voice trails off.

"It would make the mer angry if I showed up," I say. I don't fully blame them. Humans have polluted the oceans and made the waters unclean. Many mer have died. They don't trust humans, which means they don't trust me.

"I'm sorry," Lulu whispers.

"Yeah, so am I," I mutter. "Where is this dance, anyway? Near the *Clemmons*?"

"It's not held by the canyons," Dana says. "It's at a neutral site north of the canyons. There's a big area for dancing and lots of caves where we can sleep."

"Huh," I say. I look over my shoulder. I can't see my cliffs from here, but I'm close to home. "When is the dance?"

"In four days," Nari says, sounding miserable.

I've heard enough. "I'm going home."

"India, we're sorry," Dana calls after me.

"Wait," I say, as a terrible thought pops into my head. "Is Evan going?"

My friends all squirm.

"Yeah," Lulu says at last. "He's going with Melody."

The news hits me like a fist to my stomach. Melody. She's got long blond hair and huge eyes. She's liked Evan for a long time. I always thought he didn't like her. I suppose I was wrong.

"Okay, then," I say, fighting back tears. "I'll see you later. With the weather report."

I swim back to the cliffs alone, and I don't look back.

CHAPTER 3

I'm soaking wet when I get out of the water. The air has turned cooler. I shiver as I climb down the cliffs. A little boy is staring at me.

"Oh, where did you come from?" I gasp, putting my hand to my chest.

The boy looks as if he's three or four, with a dark mop of hair and large brown eyes. He is chewing on a beach towel.

I glance up and down the shore. There are a few people in the distance. I don't see anyone who's looking for a child, though.

"Where's your mum?" I ask.

The boy shakes his head.

"What's your name?" I ask.

He drops the towel from his mouth. "Nando," he says.

"Nando?" I ask. "Okay, um, where's your dad?"

Nando shrugs. I come down the last few steps to the beach. As the water dries on my skin, I get even colder. My bag is where I left it, minus the towel. I look at Nando.

"Where did you get that towel? Nando? Can you tell me?" I ask.

Nando just looks at me.

"Mine," he says, clutching the towel.

I hold out my hand. "Can I have my towel back?"

Nando shakes his head and backs up. His sandals sink into the sand.

I'm trembling now. "Look, Nando. My name's India. And that's my towel. I'm freezing. Can I have it back?" I try to ignore the fact that a corner of the towel is soaked from Nando's spit.

Nando shakes his head again. I take a step towards him, up the beach. He steps back again.

"This is silly," I mutter.

I lunge for the towel, grabbing an end. My plan is to pull it gently from Nando. His plan is to start shrieking at the top of his lungs.

"Mummy!" he yells. "Mummy! She took my towel! It's mine!"

A woman runs up to us. Her dark hair swings around her shoulders. "What's happening?" she asks. She speaks with a slight accent.

"Mine!" Nando is screaming.

"I didn't mean...," I blabber. "I really didn't mean to scare him. It's not his towel. I mean, it's mine and..."

Nando's mum gives me a tired smile and puts her hands on her son's shoulders. "I think I know what's happening here," she says. She gazes into Nando's eyes. "Fernando, where did you get that towel?"

"Mine," Nando says. He sticks his tongue out at me.

"No, it's not," I say, but Nando's mum waves me away.

"Nando, it's not your towel. It's this nice girl's towel. Isn't it?" she asks. Her voice is so patient.

"Um," Nando says.

"And now you're going to give it back to the nice girl. And we're going back to the cottage for breakfast," Nando's mum says. "We've got chocolate croissants."

"Chocolate?" Nando says, his eyes bright. The towel falls from his hands.

"Nando, give it to her, okay?" his mum says.

Nando reaches down and grabs the towel. His fist is sticky with sand as he thrusts the towel into my hand.

"And what do we say?" his mum prompts.

"Sorry," Nando says, not looking at me.

"It's okay," I say. I shake out the towel and start heading back up the beach.

Nando's words stop me. "Mummy, she's a mermaid," he says.

"She's a what?" his mum asks, half listening.

Nando tugs her hand and turns her around. "A mermaid," he says.

His mum pats his head. "Silly boy," she says. "Mermaids have tails. She has legs."

I hold out one of my legs for Nando to see. "Not a mermaid," I say. A tiny bit of fear runs up my spine.

"But I saw her," Nando insists. "Coming from there." He points at the base of the rocks that jut into the water. The same rocks where I meet my friends. The same rocks that are dangerous for human swimmers.

Nando's mum glances at me. "You came from there?" she says, pointing at the waves crashing against the base of the rocks.

"No," I say.

Nando's mum looks up and down the beach. I see the question forming on her face. "Well, where did you come from?" she asks. "I didn't see you earlier."

"There," I say, pointing in the general direction of Grandpa's cottage.

Nando's mum follows my finger. "No," she says. "I came from that direction. I didn't see you there." She glances again at the rocks.

"I was on the rocks for a little bit," I say quickly. "I know I'm not supposed to be there."

"No, you're not," she says. "It's dangerous."

"I know," I say.

Nando's mum glances up and down the beach. "Are you out here by yourself?" She takes a step towards me. "Are you okay, sweetie? Do you need any help?"

"I'm fine. My grandpa lives over there," I say, pointing in the direction of the cottage again. "Really. I'm fine."

Nando's mum looks at me for a long time. She senses that something's not quite right, but she doesn't know what. "Well, take care then," she says with a final nod.

"You too," I say.

Finally, she takes Nando's hand and walks him up the beach.

I watch them leave, feeling a chill. Nando is only a child. No one would believe him if he insisted I was a mermaid. But it might raise some questions.

I'll have to be more careful when I'm out here. I can't risk people seeing me coming in and out of the water. People can't think there are mermaids. If they do, they will search for them. The mer will be afraid and angry. The dome covering them will weaken. And the mer will have to move.

And they'll hate me forever. I don't even want to think about that happening.

I push thoughts of Nando and his mum out of my head as I walk back towards Grandpa's cottage. My clothes are soaked, and I need to grab my phone. I'm glad Grandpa is out at work so I don't have to answer any of his questions.

Twenty minutes later I'm back, walking down the beach towards town. The sun is bright. I slip my sunglasses over my eyes. The sound of the waves follows me.

The town Grandpa lives in is more like a village. Less than two thousand people live here. Almost all of them are white. When I'm in town, I'm very aware of my darker skin. How it sets me apart.

It shouldn't matter that I'm biracial. But it bugs some people. It always has. Back in Birmingham, I've been followed around in shops by salespeople too many times. But my white friends never get bothered.

Once, when I was five, I got called the N-word when I was at the playground. A man drove past and yelled it at me in front of everyone. To make matters worse, it turned out that he's the dad of one of my classmates.

Most of my friends are cool. We talk about race and racism. My family and I talk about it a lot too. I'm proud of my brown skin. I'm proud of who I am. But sometimes it feels as if the rest of the world has some catching up to do.

That's why going to town always makes me nervous. Most people know I'm Adam Finch's granddaughter. Grandpa is respected in town. Still, I can't help feel eyes on me as I walk down the narrow pavements.

Grandpa says it's a small-town thing. Everyone knows everyone, so anyone not from here gets stares. But sometimes it feels as if I get stares because of my skin colour. Grandpa patted my hand when I told him.

"Just ignore them," he said. "No matter why you think they're staring. That's what I've always done."

I shake off the feeling as best I can. The door to the Lucky Lobster clangs shut behind me. I look around the musty space, a combination bowling alley, bar, cafe and shop. It's the only place in town with decent mobile reception. And there are huge TV screens everywhere. I'll get all the news I need here.

"Can I help you with something?" a voice asks. My eyes are adjusting to the dim lighting, so I can't see who's talking to me.

"Um, just trying to get mobile reception," I say.

"Are you gonna buy something?" the voice demands. I can finally make out the person who's talking now. A white lady watches me from behind the counter. She's probably my mum's age. And she's frowning at me.

"Uh, yes," I say. I grab a pack of chewing gum from a display. A cooler hums behind me. I turn around, slide the heavy door open, and take out a sweating bottle of iced tea.

"Is that all?" the lady asks as I put my items down on the counter. Her eyes narrow at me.

"Why?" I reply. "Is there a minimum purchase rule or something?" I hold the lady's gaze. I'm not going to back down.

With a huff, she punches the buttons of the till. I hand her my money, and she gives me my change. I count it quickly before sliding it into my pocket.

"You're Jamal's girl," the woman says suddenly.

"Yeah," I say, surprised. Most people know my grandpa, but almost no one talks about my dad. "Do you know him?"

Her eyes soften. "Used to," she says.

I wait to see if she is going to say more. When she goes back to her crossword puzzle, I walk away towards the empty bowling lanes.

Banks of televisions cover the walls. Usually the Lucky Lobster is showing a mix of sports shows and events. But now every single TV is tuned to the weather station. And every screen displays a huge, angry, swirling mass churning towards Cornwall.

The storm.

"Whoa," I whisper.

"It's a big one," the lady says, right over my shoulder. She has crept up on me, making me jump.

"You scared me," I say.

"It's heading right towards us," she says. "Wiping me out of supplies."

I look around the shop part of the Lucky Lobster. Most of the shelves are bare.

"I'm out of bottled water, bread, torches and tins of soup," the woman says. She pushes a stringy piece of hair out of her face. "People always go for the soup during a big storm."

"Um, okay," I reply.

"Your granddad hasn't been in for supplies though," she says.

"He was waiting to see what happened," I say. He hoped the storm would burn out before it reached us."

The woman slides me a look. "Well, that's not going to happen now," she says. "It grew suddenly."

We stand there in silence for a while, watching the storm creep across the ocean. It's going to be bad. I need to tell my friends.

As I'm leaving, my eyes fall on a painting hanging behind the desk. A woman sits on a rock, enjoying the sun. Her hair falls over her bare shoulders. And her tail floats in the water.

I've seen countless pictures of mermaids in the tourist shops. This one is different. I walk closer, squinting my eyes. Then I notice. The mermaid's eyes have been scratched out.

The woman grabs my arm.

"If you're Jamal's daughter, you know about them," she hisses in my ear. "But I'd think twice about warning them. They deserve their fate. All of them. They deserve to die."

I pull my arm free of her grip.

"What are you talking about?" I ask.

But I get no answer. The bell over the door rings as another customer comes in. The woman turns her back on me. I leave the Lucky Lobster confused and upset.

CHAPTER 4

"It's going to be bad," I say later the same day. I hover over the waves, clinging to the rocks. My friends bob in the water beneath me. I slipped out to the rocks after I left the Lucky Lobster. There was no sign of Nando, his mum or anyone else on the beach.

"How bad?" Lulu asks.

"They're giving an amber warning right now, but it could become red by tomorrow," I say.

"What does that mean?" Dana asks.

"It's how the weather service warns us about storms," I explain. "A red warning is the worst. The storm is going to be bad. Everyone in town is preparing for it. Most of the tourists have left."

"When does it get here?" Lulu asks.

"Another couple of days," I say.

Nari twists a long strand of black hair around her finger. "We might need to cancel the dance," she says. "Move into deeper waters."

"Or head further east," Dana offers. "Maybe we could find a new place for the dance." Her voice almost sounds hopeful or upbeat.

I start to feel upset. I did all this work to find out about the storm. And my friends are worried about a dance?

Nari notices my face. "Or we could just have the dance a different time," she says. "Maybe after we convince Ani to let India come."

"The dance is the least of our concerns," Lulu says. She chews her bottom lip. "We need to tell my mum what's happening."

They turn to go. "Wait," I call, just as they are about to disappear beneath the waves.

"What is it?" Dana asks. She turns back to face me. Her red hair is plastered to her face.

"Do you know if anyone else on land knows about you?" I ask. I can't get the woman from the Lucky Lobster out of my mind.

"Knows about us? Or about mermaids in general?" Lulu asks.

"There was a woman in the shop. She knew who my family was," I explain. "She mentioned my dad in particular. Then she told me I shouldn't warn you about the storm. That you will get what you deserve."

"What did your granddad say?" Nari asks, swimming closer to the rocks.

"I haven't asked him about it yet," I say. "He's still at work."

My friends glance at each other and shake their heads. "We don't know anything about it," Dana says.

"Maybe Ani does?" I ask hopefully. "And maybe I should come with you to find out what she thinks?"

My friends look sad.

"We'll ask her about it, India," Lulu says. She comes close enough to the rocks to put her hand over mine. "We'll let you know."

"We wish you could come with us," Nari says. "But Ani says you need to stay on land. We need you to watch the weather reports."

"I know," I say. I struggle to my feet, brushing bits of sand off my backside. "I suppose I'll just have to find out for myself."

I start walking away.

"Same time tomorrow?" Nari calls after me.

"Yep," I say, but I don't look back.

I crawl over the rocks towards the beach, pausing to make sure no one can see me. I don't want to risk another Nando episode.

Turns out I don't need to worry. The beach is empty. Like I told my friends, most of the tourists have left as the storm closes in.

When I get back to the cottage, Grandpa is piling sandbags in front of the house.

"The storm got worse," I say.

"I saw," Grandpa replies.

"Has it changed course at all?" I ask, helping Grandpa lift one of the sacks.

He shakes his head. "I checked the reports just before I left work. It's going to be bad."

"Any chance it will miss us?" I ask.

"It might," Grandpa says, standing back to look at the pile of sandbags. "We should know more tomorrow."

"I talked to my friends," I tell him as we go inside the cottage.

"Good," Grandpa says. "They can move to deeper waters for safety."

I think about what my friends told me yesterday. "They said their powers are affected by storms," I say.

Grandpa is nodding. "Something about the oxygen levels in the water. Storms bring deeper water to the surface. That water has less oxygen in it, which makes the mer weaker."

"Would it affect me the same?" I ask.

Grandpa fixes his eyes on me. "You're not to go into the water when the storm hits," he says.

I grind the toe of my sandal into the floor. "I won't," I grumble. "I was just asking."

"I know what happens when you ask about something, India," Grandpa says. "It usually means you're going to do it."

I shrug and wander to the kitchen. Grandpa's right. Whenever people tell me I can't do something, I usually go ahead and do it. It drives my parents nuts, but it's who I am.

I decide to change the subject.

"Do you know the lady who works at the Lucky Lobster?" I ask, munching on some crisps.

"Why are you asking about her?" Grandpa asks.

"She said some weird things to me when I was there today," I say.

"Huh," Grandpa grunts, shuffling to his room.

"Who is she?" I call after him.

"She's no concern of ours," Grandpa says.

"But why does she hate the mer?" I ask.

At my words, Grandpa pauses. He turns slowly to look at me.

"Don't mess with her," he says. "She's dangerous."

"Who is she?" I ask again. "And how does she know about the mer?"

Grandpa drops onto the couch with a sigh. "Her name is Morgan," he says. "And she's a sea witch."

"A sea witch?" I ask. A crisp falls from my hand. "Like Ursula from *The Little Mermaid* film?"

Grandpa waves to a chair. "I don't watch films. But you'd better sit down," he says. "I'll tell you what I know. First, tell me what she said to you about the mer."

"She said I shouldn't warn them about the storm," I say. "She said that they deserve their fate. That they deserve to die." The words are cold and hard on my lips.

"That sounds like Morgan," Grandpa says.

"She knew who I was," I say. "Does she know we're part-mer?"

"She knows," Grandpa says. "She's always known." He rubs his eyes. "She and your dad used to be friends a long time ago."

"She mentioned that she knew him," I say.

"Although she didn't sound as if she hated him. Not like how she hates the mer."

"Morgan and your dad were in love once," Grandpa says.

"Oh," I say, not quite sure how to take this news. It's weird hearing about your parents' lives before they became your parents. "You said she's a sea witch? Is she part-mer too?"

"No," Grandpa says. "Witches and mermaids aren't the same thing. They are enemies, actually."

"Why?" I ask.

"Sea witches are humans who draw power from water. Most sea witches aren't very powerful. In fact, only a few of them are actual witches. The rest are just pretending," Grandpa says. "They are just playing at being witches."

It hits me that I'm talking about sea witches with Grandpa. As if it's totally normal. My life is so weird. A few months ago, I had no idea mermaids were real. What's next? Vampires?

"So then is Morgan a real witch or not?" I ask.

"Oh, she's very real," Grandpa says. "She comes from a long line of sea witches. Her mother and her mother's mother before her. All of them were very powerful witches."

"So why do they hate mermaids?" I ask.

"Even real witches like Morgan will never have the same powers as mermaids," Grandpa says.

"So they're jealous," I say.

"Yes," Grandpa says.

"And that's why Morgan wants to hurt my friends? She's jealous?" I ask.

"It's also personal for Morgan. When she and Jamal were young, Morgan felt as if she was losing your dad to the mer. I think she hoped he would turn his back on the mer and choose her," Grandpa says.

"But he didn't," I say.

"No, he didn't." Grandpa sighs. "He turned his back on the ocean. But he also turned his back on her. Moved to Birmingham. Broke her heart."

"What are Morgan's powers?" I ask. I don't want to hear more about my dad's love life.

"Morgan can control water," Grandpa says.

A thought occurs to me. "Control water? Is she making the storm happen?"

"I don't know," Grandpa says. "I don't think she's strong enough to create a storm like this. But once one started..." Grandpa's voice trails off.

"You think she could control it?" I ask.

"Maybe," Grandpa says.

"I should tell my friends," I say.

"Yes," Grandpa agrees. His knees pop as he stands. "Tomorrow. I'm going to bed."

"Goodnight, Grandpa," I say.

His bedroom door closes. I'm tired too, but I sit in the living room for a while, thinking about Morgan and sea witches. If she's controlling the storm, we're all in trouble.

CHAPTER 5

As it turns out, I don't have to worry about Morgan's powers. Grandpa returns from town the next evening with news that the storm is weakening.

"It's going to turn east and head out to sea," he says. He pours himself a cup of coffee.

"That's great news," I respond. "I can't wait to tell my friends. They'll be happy."

I feel a surge of sadness that I don't understand at first. Then I realize what it is. If the storm goes away, they can have their dance, I think. And Evan will be there with Melody. And I'm not invited.

I choke down my sadness and look around for something to do.

"I can help you move the sandbags if you like, Grandpa," I offer.

Grandpa shakes his head. "We'll leave them for a few days."

"Really?" I ask. "But won't they get in the way? And you said the storm is getting weaker."

"Even a weak storm can cause flooding this close to shore," Grandpa says. "And there's always a chance it will strengthen again and head back this way."

"Do you think it will?" I ask.

"Probably not," Grandpa says. "But you can't be sure."

"What should I tell the mermaids, then?" I ask.

"Tell them what you know; the storm is weakening and heading out to sea," he says. "It's hundreds of miles south from the canyons. They will want to stay on their guard, but they should be fine."

My heart sinks to my stomach. I mentally kick myself. I shouldn't be hoping for a storm in order to see my friends. I should be happy that they will be safe.

"I'm going to talk to them now," I say, checking the clock ticking over the kitchen sink.

"Watch the time, India. It will be dark soon," Grandpa says.

The front door bangs shut behind me. I'm halfway down the path when I feel eyes on the back of my neck. I turn quickly, scanning the underbrush. No one's there.

"Just your imagination, India," I tell myself.

I look around the entire time I'm walking to the beach. I still don't see anyone, but I can't shake the feeling that someone is following me. I also can't shake the idea that it might be Morgan, the sea witch.

When I reach the beach, I don't see anyone. No Nando, no tourists, no sea witch. I suppose I should be relieved, but instead I feel creeped out.

The feeling lasts until I climb over the black rocks. When I'm out of sight from the beach, I find a smooth patch of rock and settle down to wait for my friends.

I don't wait long before three heads pop out of the water. I find myself searching for a fourth head, hoping that for some reason Evan is with them. He's not.

"What's the latest?" Lulu asks, getting right to the point. "Do we need to move to different waters?"

"It's good news," I say. "The storm is weakening and heading east."

Dana claps her hands. "That is good news!"

"How far east?" Lulu asks.

"Grandpa says it will stay south of the canyons," I tell them.

This time even Lulu smiles. "Very good news."

"We can have the dance!" Nari exclaims.

My friends all shriek happily. Then Dana catches sight of my face. "Oh, sorry," she says.

"We asked Ani again if you could come," Nari says.

"And?" I ask.

Lulu shakes her head. Her hair has been braided, dozens of thin coils waving around her ears.

"She says it's still too dangerous," she says.

"But that was before she knew the storm wouldn't be a problem," Nari counters. "Maybe she'll change her mind."

"Yeah, maybe," Lulu says, her face brightening. "We should get back to her as soon as we can."

"Come back and see me soon?" I ask, my voice breaking.

Nari swims over to the rock and reaches her hands up. I bend down, and we hug.

"Of course," she says. "We'll come back as soon as we can."

The others swim over and hug me too. My top is damp by the time we're done hugging.

"Oh, wait," I say, catching them right before they leave. "What do you know about sea witches?"

Lulu's face scrunches. "Sea witches? There are some legends, I think, but I don't know much about them," she says.

"They live on land, right?" Dana says. "Humans?"

"That's what Grandpa says," I respond.

"Why are you asking about it?" Nari says. "Oh wait, is this because of the woman who said weird things to you?"

"Morgan," I say. "Grandpa says she's a sea witch. And that she hates mermaids."

Lulu approaches. "Can she hurt us?"

"I don't know," I say. "Grandpa says she's not strong enough to create a storm. But if one got started, she could control it."

"This storm got weaker, though," Lulu points out. "So doesn't that mean this Morgan person isn't behind it?"

"I suppose," I say.

"Well, that's good news," Dana says.

Nari puts her hand on Dana's shoulder. "We should tell Ani about her, though," she says.

"Yep," Lulu agrees. "She'll want to know right away. We need to get home."

"See you soon," I say.

We all hug again. And then they're gone. They disappear into the ocean.

My sadness returns as I pick my way carefully over the slick rocks. I walk towards the forest. I sit under a huge tree, leaning against the rough bark. The tree feels solid and secure. I feel safe.

Until the voice comes out of the shadows.

"Didn't I tell you they deserve their fate?"

I squeak and jump. "Who's there?" I demand.

A face appears before me. Pale, framed by dirty blond hair.

"Morgan," I whisper.

A glimmer of recognition lights her face. "So, your grandfather told you about me."

"What do you want?" I say. I try to hold my shaking legs steady.

"I told you to stay away from those ... those beasts," she spits.

Her words make me angry. My legs are no longer shaking as fury rises within me.

"They are not beasts!" I shout.

Morgan snorts. "They are beasts who deserve their fate." She looks me up and down. "And so are you."

She looks as if she's expecting me to run away. Instead I take a step towards her.

"I am not a beast," I spit. "And neither are they. You leave us alone."

Morgan holds my eyes for a long moment. Then she dips her head in a faint nod. "I will be seeing you, India Finch." There's an edge in her eyes. "Better watch yourself."

With that she turns and walks away.

"Are you behind the storm?" I call after her. "Wait! Answer me!"

The forest swallows her. For a moment I think she has simply disappeared, but I can still hear her footsteps along the shore. Eventually the sound fades.

"You'd better watch yourself," I whisper. My fists are clenched at my side.

It might be my imagination, but I hear mocking laughter following me all the way back to the cottage.

CHAPTER 6

Over the next few days, the storm continues to weaken. I try not to think about my friends. Instead, I keep myself busy.

One day, I clean the cottage from top to bottom. The next day I tackle the garden, pulling weeds from the rocky soil. I reread Toni Morrison's *Beloved* while lying on the beach. I even help Grandpa at the marine museum where he volunteers. I spend my day stapling brochures together and come home with paper cuts all over my hands.

Since I can't heal myself on land, I dip into the ocean to fix my cuts. I have to dive deep to activate my mer powers. I hold my right hand over a gash on my left thumb. I picture the cut healing. Power flows from my fingers into my own skin. The cut disappears.

And every day I look for a seaweed wreath.

"They're not calling me," I complain to Grandpa one afternoon. He's just come home from work. I have veggie burgers ready to cook. All I need is for Grandpa to light the grill on his ancient oven.

Grandpa drops heavily into his chair. "You need to go to them," he says.

"I mean, I know they're busy–" I start. Then Grandpa's words register. "Wait, what?"

Grandpa rubs his eyes. "The storm is getting worse," he says.

I drop the rolls I was holding. They bounce on the counter. "It's getting worse? But a few days ago you said it was weakening! You said so yesterday, in fact."

"Sometimes storms hit pockets of warmer water. They gain strength," Grandpa says.

"How bad is it?" I ask, sinking into a chair.

"The weather service is calling it a super storm," Grandpa says. "It's heading straight for us."

"What about the canyons?" I ask. Panic is building inside me. "You said I need to tell the mer."

"The storm is going to go right over the canyons before it reaches us," Grandpa says. "They need to be warned."

I'm on my feet and halfway out of the door before Grandpa calls me back. "India, wait," he says.

"There's no time to wait!" I shout, catching the front door with my foot.

Grandpa waves me back inside. "There's more you need to know before you go running off to them," he says

"Fine," I say, stepping back inside the cottage. The door slams shut behind me. "What is it?"

Grandpa grabs a pen and paper. "I'll draw you a map of where they think the storm will go," he says.

His pen moves over the paper in quick strokes. The coastline appears beneath his hands. He describes where the storm is likely to hit.

I can't take the map with me into the water. I study it until I have it memorized.

"Got it," I say, standing to leave.

Grandpa's hand closes over my wrist. "There's one more thing, India."

His eyes look so serious that for a moment I think someone's died. "What is it?" I ask.

"The storm. It's had some help getting stronger," he says.

"Morgan?" I ask. "How do you know?"

Grandpa sighs, and his shoulders slouch. "I was out for a walk late last night. Couldn't sleep. I came around a bend and saw Morgan at the edge of the ocean. She had her arms in the air. Lightning shot from her fingers. I felt a huge burst of energy roll across the water, away from the beach. I think she was making the storm stronger."

"Did she see you?" I ask.

Grandpa shakes his head. "I stayed out of sight. Morgan is dangerous to us and the mer," he says.

"What are we going to do about her?" I ask.

"Nothing," Grandpa says.

"You're going to let her get away with this?" I cry.

Grandpa looks at me. "I'm going to talk to her. Tomorrow, maybe," he says. "But what you're going to do is visit the mer. Tell them what's happening. Keep them safe."

"Okay," I say. I want to confront Morgan myself, but warning my friends is more important. "I'll go right now."

"It will be dark in a few hours, India," Grandpa points out.

"It only takes an hour to get to the canyons," I say.

Grandpa lays his hand on the table next to his map. "And how will you find the canyons?"

I bite back a bunch of swear words. "I don't know," I say at last. My head drops into my hands. "I hadn't thought about it. Sometimes they're waiting for me, even though they haven't called me."

I hope Grandpa can't see the blush on my cheeks. Evan's the one who sometimes waits for me. Maybe he'll be there now.

"You need to go to them," Grandpa agrees. "But you need to get there safely. You'll never find the canyons on your own. The dome will hide them from you."

"I know all of this!" I shout. "But I have to go and tell them. I can't wait."

"Wait until dawn," Grandpa says.

"I can't wait that long," I say. "I'll be swimming into a storm anyway, won't I? I should go sooner."

Grandpa runs a hand over his cropped hair. "I don't like it," he says. "But you have a point."

"Why don't you come with me?" I suggest.

"If it was calm water, I'd go. But I'm not that strong a swimmer," Grandpa says. "You can make it, though. I've seen you swim."

"So I can go?" I ask.

"Yes," Grandpa says with a sigh. "I trust you. But come back in an hour if you haven't found them. Come back before the storm hits."

"What if it comes faster than I can swim back?" I ask.

"Then I suppose you should stay with the mer. They'll take care of you," Grandpa says.

I jump up and give Grandpa a quick hug, which surprises both of us. We're not huggers. "Thanks, Grandpa," I say. "When are you going to see Morgan?"

"I'll go now," Grandpa says, struggling to his feet. His knees crack as he stands. "Hopefully I can stop her somehow. Make her stop the storm before it gets to Cornwall. And before it gets to the canyons. Then you don't have to worry about getting back."

Excitement fills me, which is odd, I suppose. A sea witch is sending a storm to the mer. And I'm about to swim into stormy waters. But I get to see my friends and be with my underwater family. I get to help keep them safe.

Feeling happy, I give Grandpa another hug, then run down the path to the beach.

CHAPTER 7

I kick off from the rocks and swim east. I've been to Ice Canyon enough times that I remember the path. I take a left at the hill shaped like a dog. I take another left at the orange rocks.

Half an hour later I swim through the two spears of rock. The canyons are nearby. The problem is, I can't see them. My only hope is that a guard finds me. Otherwise I might be lost out here.

The last light of day is fading from the water. I stop near a purple sea cave.

"I'll stay the night if no one finds me," I say to no one in particular.

My teeth start chattering. It's not cold. I'm just worried no one will find me. It is creepy out here, all by myself.

"Someone will find you, India," I say aloud. "I'm sure."

I wish my voice sounded less scared. I peer into the mouth of the cave. All I see are shadows.

Wait, did something move?

"Snap out of it, India. Stop talking to yourself," I say. "And remember? This is why you don't watch horror movies. You get too scared. You think everything is a ghost. Or a vampire." I glance over my shoulder, feeling as if someone's watching me. "Or a mermaid-eating shark."

I stop talking. I move into the mouth of the cave. The shadows don't move.

"Good," I say. "Wait, I wasn't going to keep talking. So I'm going to stop now."

My voice echoes in the cave. It's fully dark now. I can't see a thing.

"Perfect," I say into the darkness.

"What's perfect?" a raspy voice replies.

I scream so loud that I'm sure Grandpa can hear me back home.

"Who's there?" I demand. I push myself against the wall of the cave. "Who's there?" I ask again.

I hear a shuffle and a clunk. Is it a shark? A giant squid? But wait, sharks and giant squid can't talk. Then I hear a low groan and a few swear words.

"Hit my head against the overhang when you screamed," the voice says. It sounds familiar.

"Bruce?" I ask, edging away from the wall. Bruce is an Ice Canyon guard. And one of the few mer who actually likes me.

"Yeah, it's me," Bruce says. "Hang on a second." There's some rummaging sounds and another thunk.

"Dang it, hit my elbow that time," Bruce mutters.

Light flickers and coats the inside of the cave. Bruce, the gruff Ice Canyon guard, is floating in the middle of the cave. He's grinning, which makes his eyes crinkle.

"Knew I had one of these somewhere," he says. He holds up a jellyfish. "Now, what in the heck are you doing out here, India Finch? Not that I'm not glad to see you. But last I checked, you're not supposed to come here on your own."

"I have news," I say. "About the storm."

Bruce's kind eyes look worried. "The storm? Last we heard it wasn't going to be a problem."

"Things changed," I say. "It hit some warm water. And there's a sea witch ... it's a long story."

"A sea witch?" Bruce asks. His voice drops. "Who?"

"Her name is Morgan. She lives in the town where Grandpa lives," I explain.

Bruce swallows hard. His face falls into shadows. "Morgan," he says. "There's a name I didn't think I'd hear again."

"You know her?" I ask.

Bruce shakes his head. "I don't know her personally, but I know of her. She gave us some trouble a few years back. Right about the time your dad visited us."

"Yeah, she said something about that," I say. "She also said she wants to hurt all of the mer. That's why Grandpa thinks she might be behind the storm getting stronger."

"Well, if Morgan's involved, that's not good," Bruce says. "Come on. I'll take you into the canyons. No one's there right now. They're all at the dance site."

"The dance is today?" I ask.

"Tomorrow. But it's too far to go tonight. You can sleep in your friends' cave. We'll head out in the morning," Bruce says.

Ice Canyon is only a few minutes away. I follow Bruce and the faint light of the jellyfish.

"What were you doing out here?" I ask.

"Patrolling the area," Bruce says. "It's my night to work."

"Why aren't you at the dance?" I ask.

Bruce laughs, a low, rusty sound. "I'm too old for a dance," he says. "Had too many of them already in my life. Time for some peace and quiet."

"Okay," I say, although I think he's nuts. I'd trade peace and quiet for a party any day.

When we reach Ice Canyon, it's empty. I'm not surprised. It's just strange to see it like this. I'm used to all of the mer coming out to glare at me whenever I arrive.

"Everyone's at the dance?" I ask.

"Most of them," Bruce says. "There's a few more like me hanging around. Otherwise, they're gone."

The caves are dark and quiet. The water presses around us from all sides, like a blanket. I can see why Bruce thinks it's peaceful.

"Well, see you tomorrow," I say once we reach my friends' cave.

"Bright and early," he replies, giving me a wave before swimming away.

When I'm alone in the cave, it seems less peaceful. I miss my friends. I can picture them here, all the fun we've had. All of the late-night talks. Now it's just me.

Feeling lonely, I settle against the wall and try to sleep.

When I wake up, the sun is bright. I feel happy, knowing I'll see my friends today. I stretch my arms and swim out of the cave.

"I'm ready!" I call to Bruce, who is frowning. "What is it?" I ask.

"Look," he says. I glance to where he's pointing. The sunlight is fading. Dark, churning water is heading towards us.

"Is that the storm?" I ask with dread.

"It's the outer edge of it," Bruce says. "We need to get going."

"Okay," I say.

I follow Bruce out of the canyon. Behind us, the storm keeps coming, following us all the way north.

CHAPTER 8

The storm follows us all day. It's fast, but we swim faster. Still, the ocean gets darker the further north we swim. By the time we're almost at the dance site, the currents are getting stronger.

I still hold out hope that Grandpa will change Morgan's mind. My hope is fading, though, as the waters get stronger.

"Are we almost there?" I ask. I barely get the words out before a current of water knocks me to one side.

"You okay?" Bruce asks. He's struggling to swim in the stronger currents too.

"Fine," I say. "Well, not fine. I'm freezing."

"That's part of the storm," Bruce explains. "Cold water gets stirred up from the deep. It'll be better once we get to the dance."

"Why?" I ask.

"You'll see," he says, swimming ahead.

"Can't you just tell me?" I call, following him around a bend. We're swimming up the side of a rocky slope.

Bruce reaches the top of the slope and grins at me. "Why don't I just show you?"

I swim to where he is. Then I start to laugh.

We're on the top of an old volcano. Below us, in a large crater, is the mer dance.

Jellyfish hover over the dance floor, lighting the area with a soft glow. A few of them are blinking in time to a pulsing beat. A mer band plays in one corner, beating on drums made of shells.

There must be hundreds of mer at the dance. Most of them are on the dance floor, spinning and swaying. The dance floor is a blur of colours. Everyone's tails are dazzling under the jellyfish light.

In the swirl of bodies, I catch a flash of red hair and a streak of black hair. Dana and Nari are dancing together, their hands held tight. They are smiling at each other. For the first time I wonder if they feel more than friendship for each other. The thought makes me happy.

I look for Lulu and see her dancing with a merman with an orange tail. Ropes of pearls hang from her head. She looks beautiful.

The song comes to an end, and a new one starts. Lulu spins to a new partner. Dana and Nari keep dancing together. I can't wait to go down and talk to them.

I just wish I wasn't wearing an old top and skirt. I suppose swimming in a dress would have been impossible. But still, I wish I were a little bit dressed up.

"Seen enough?" Bruce asks. "We do have a job to do, after all."

"Oh, right," I say, remembering the storm. "Do you see Ani? Or Storm, even?"

Bruce eyes the crowd as we make our way down the slope to the dance floor. "There," he says, pointing at a group of mer on the far side of the crater.

"Of course they're as far away as possible," I grumble. "Let's go."

It's not easy to work my way through the crowded floor. I'm lost in a swirl of tails. Someone grabs my hands and tries to pull me into a dance. I shake off his hands and keep swimming towards Ani.

I glance behind me, but I've lost sight of Bruce. I don't see any sign of Nari, Dana or Lulu, either. Suddenly I feel very alone, even though I'm in the middle of a crowd.

"Move, please!" I shout. But my voice gets swallowed up by the pounding beat.

Then other hands cover mine. A face floats in front of mine. Dark eyes, brown sugar skin.

"Evan?" I gasp.

"India!" he says. "What are you doing here?"

"Yes, what are you doing here, India?" a cool voice asks. A white arm lays itself over Evan's shoulders.

Ugh, Melody, I think. She probably hasn't let Evan out of her sight all night.

"If I remember, you're not supposed to be here," Melody says. "Not unless you've been called for. Which you haven't."

"I don't have any time for your games, Melody," I tell the blond mermaid. I feel a glimmer of happiness when Evan shakes off Melody's arm. "I need to warn Ani and Storm."

"About what?" Evan asks, frowning.

"The storm," I say. I wave at the dark sky behind me. Even Melody looks concerned as she notices the dark waters.

"I thought we were safe," Evan says.

"It changed course," I explain. "Long story. But I need to talk to Ani. Or your dad."

We're in the middle of the dance floor. It feels as if we're miles and miles from Ani and Storm.

Evan takes my hand. "Let's go," he says.

It takes us forever to get across the floor. There are so many dancing mer blocking our way.

I'm glad Evan and I are holding hands. If we weren't, I would have lost him several times.

By the time we reach Ani and Storm, I've been elbowed four times. My legs sting from where I got smacked by someone's tail. It was accidental, but it still hurts.

Ani's braids float around her head as she nods in time to the music. She doesn't notice us at first. I have to tug on her hand.

"India?" she gasps when she sees me. "What are you doing here?"

"You are not supposed to be here," Storm growls, glaring at me.

"Lighten up, Dad," Evan says.

Storm stares at his son. "What did you just say to me?" His eyes land on our hands, which are still clasped. He looks as if he wants to vomit.

"I'm telling you to leave India alone," Evan says. "She's not trying to hurt us. She's here to warn us!"

"Warn us? About what?" Ani asks.

At that moment, shadows falls over the dance floor. The water temperature drops, and the music dims.

"What's happening?" Ani asks.

"The storm," I blurt out.

Ani is shaking her head. "We're not supposed to get a storm. It's heading away from us. You said so yourself."

"A few days ago it was heading away," I say. "But things changed. Now it's heading straight towards the canyons."

Ani looks relieved. "But we're miles from the canyons. We'll just stay here for a few days before going home."

Storm lays his hand on Ani's shoulder. "That's not going to be possible," he says. "Look."

The waters have darkened over the top of the crater. Underneath the drone of the music, I can hear a distant rumble.

"The storm is huge," I say. "I'm not entirely sure where we are right now. But it's possible we're still in it's path."

"No," Ani whispers, but it is a prayer more than a command. Even Ani cannot change the course of a super storm. "We'll lose our powers," she murmurs.

I remember what Lulu said, that mer powers get weaker when there's a storm.

"There's a sea witch," I explain, talking fast. "Back home. We think she's behind it. Grandpa's trying to change Morgan's mind, but I'm not sure he will be able to."

"What did you say?" Ani asks, her voice snapping.

"Which part?" I ask.

"The part about the sea witch. You said her name," Ani says.

"Morgan," I say. "I just met her a few days ago. She hates the mer, though."

Ani nods and her eyes have a faraway look. "Yes, she does."

"You know her?" I ask.

"It was a long time ago," Ani says.

The rumbling is getting louder. Without even thinking about it, I inch closer to Evan.

He puts his arm around my shoulders, drawing me against him. It's a romantic gesture, but right now I'm just glad I'm not alone.

"What do we do?" Storm asks, looking at Ani. I've never heard him sound scared, like he does now. It makes me scared too.

"Shelter," she whispers, "we need shelter." Ani takes Storm's hand and swims to the centre of the floor. "Take cover!" she shouts. "All mer need to take cover now! To the trenches! The storm is almost here!"

She lets go of Storm and starts herding people off the dance floor. Storm does the same. The mer flee, stirring up the water as they go.

"Everyone has to go calmly!" Ani shouts.

The water becomes so churned that suddenly I can't see anything. I reach out blindly. A wave sweeps me to one side. I tumble head over heels. By the time I've righted myself, I realize I've lost Evan.

"Evan!" I shout. I picture my friends lost in the storm, and it makes me feel sick. "Dana! Nari! Lulu! Where are you guys?"

I hear a few shouts. The water clears enough for me to see I'm on the dance floor. I see a flash of green and blue. Then purple. Someone bumps me from behind. I reach out, but I don't catch anyone's hand.

The rumble is as loud as a train. The crater walls are shaking.

I need to get to a cave.

It's the last thought that runs through my mind before the storm hits.

CHAPTER 9

The water erupts around me, cold and churning. Sand fills my mouth. I can't see my hand in front of my face. A dark shape hurtles towards me.

Is it Evan? Another mer?

No, it's a huge rock!

I duck at the last minute. The rock misses me by just a few inches.

"Evan!" I shriek. The water sweeps my words away.

I'm picked up and shaken, turned upside down like a snow globe. The walls of the crater flash past my face. If I don't grab something, I'm going to be swept into the deep sea.

I stretch out my arm. The force of a thousand waves pushes it back against my body. The water is so strong I'm afraid it will rip my hand off. I kick my legs. I need shelter.

Another wave comes, knocking me over. I twist and tumble.

Which way is up?

What am I going to do?

Am I going to die out here?

The currents slow for a moment. The water clears briefly. It's long enough for me to get my bearings.

I see the side of a cliff. A dark cave yawns open. It's about six feet away from me. I have to get into that cave. It's my only hope.

I kick my legs as hard as I can. My arms slice through the water. The rumbling gets even louder. The waters grow darker. Another current hits me.

"No!" I scream. I watch as the cave gets further away. The water takes me into the middle of the crater.

Suddenly I feel angry. I'm not going to let this be the end. I'm not going to die out here.

"You aren't going to beat me!" I scream. "I'm not going to let you win!"

I'm shouting at the storm. Which is useless, since the storm doesn't care. It won't stop just because I'm yelling at it.

Morgan's face floats into my mind, stringy blond hair framing angry eyes. My anger finds a new target.

"I'm not going to let you kill me!" I shout at the image. "And I'm not going to let you hurt my friends! Just you wait!"

Two currents tug at me. I kick my legs again, swimming towards a looming shape. I hope it's the wall of the crater. I pull free of the currents. I'm almost at the wall.

Then I get swept away again.

"No!" I scream.

"Don't fight it!" a voice says. Hands grip my arm. "Wait for the right moment," the voice says in my ear. "Do you understand?"

"Yes!" I shout, nodding my head at the same time.

"Good. Now go!" the voice shouts.

The currents relax for a moment. I can see the crater wall before me. In that pause, I turn and swim towards it. The hands on my arm fall away. I'm not swimming alone, however. Whoever helped me is following me to the wall.

"In here!" the voice shouts.

The currents are picking up again. Sand scrapes my face. I reach out for the wall, find an opening and duck into the safety of a cave.

Evan tumbles in behind me.

"It was you?" I ask. I reach for his hands to pull him further into the cave. "You saved me?"

Evan smiles a crooked smile. "We saved each other," he says.

I don't get a chance to say more. At that moment, there's a huge roar. The cave shakes as the storm gets even stronger.

Then a pile of rocks comes down on top of Evan.

"No!" I shout. I'm sobbing as I fling myself towards the rocks. "No!"

Now that the entrance is sealed, the cave is completely dark. I can't see a thing. All I can do is run my hands over the rocks, trying to find Evan.

The rocks are rough beneath my hands. I find the edge of where they've fallen. Sand gets jammed beneath my fingernails. I trace the edge of the rock. With each sweep of my hands, I'm afraid I'll find pieces of flesh and sticky blood.

I'm sobbing, the sounds bouncing off the cave walls. Outside the storm is still raging. More rocks pound against the cave wall. The roar is deafening.

I'm so cold. My teeth are chattering, my arms trembling. I can see my fingers shake.

"Wait," I whisper. I glance over my shoulder. A tiny jellyfish is bobbing in the cave, sending out a dim light.

"Thank you," I say.

I look back at the rock pile. And then I see Evan.

He was thrown clear of the rockslide. He lies on his side about three feet from the pile. I was searching in the wrong place.

"Evan!" I cry, swimming over to him. "Evan, it's India! Wake up!"

My hands are on his arms, his face.

"Evan? Evan!" I say. I repeat his name, as if it will magically wake him up.

Instead he lies with his eyes closed, a trickle of blood trailing from his forehead. Even in this light his skin looks pale.

"Evan," I murmur. I note his injuries. He's got a few cuts and scrapes on his arms and legs. The cut on his head is long but shallow. He's also got a big bump on his head. My biggest concern is that he's still knocked out.

"Don't worry, I'll save you," I say, holding out my hands.

There's a slight buzzing sound at the top of my head, but I ignore it. It's probably just more storm noise. The water has gotten even colder. I'm shaking hard. Even still, I hold my hands as still as possible. I call forth my healing powers.

Nothing happens.

I give my hands a shake. I take a deep breath. And I hold out my hands again.

"I will heal you, Evan," I murmur.

Once again, nothing happens.

"Okay, India, it's just a fluke. You can do this," I tell myself. I shake out my shoulders this time. The buzzing in my head gets louder. Stars prick the edge of my vision.

"What's happening?" I ask the jellyfish. Since it's a jellyfish, it doesn't answer.

I start to laugh. This is a bad sign. I must be going into shock or something.

"Nope, not going to happen," I say, slapping my cheek. "Stay awake, India."

I hold out my hands again. I channel my healing powers. I wait for them to emerge.

But nothing happens.

Then I remember – storms can wipe out mer powers. I can't heal Evan.

"Crap," I say.

I sit back on my heels. I'm shaking from both the cold and from knowing I can't help Evan. "What am I going to do?" I whimper.

Images from my CPR class and lifeguard training flitter through my head.

"That's right, you've done first aid, India Finch," I tell myself. I probably shouldn't be talking so much. I should save my energy. But the sound of my voice is keeping me from freaking out right now.

"You know how to help him," I say. "So do it."

I crouch next to Evan, feeling for a pulse. My hands skim over his throat. His skin is clammy. I can feel a faint flutter at the base of his neck.

"Evan," I murmur, trying to wake him. I say it louder: "Evan. Wake up."

Nothing.

"Well, good that he's not bleeding more," I say. "Not so good about the lump on his head." Only the jellyfish hears me.

I hold my ear over Evan's mouth. After a few moments I realize I'm listening for breath.

"Not air, India," I tell myself. "Water."

I hold my fingers in front of his mouth. I can feel a faint trickle of water going in and out of his mouth. I move my hands back to his throat. His pulse is still weak.

"Okay, what next?" I say, trying to remember my first-aid training. At some point I'm supposed to call for emergency medical help.

"Yeah, that's not going to happen," I say. "No ambulances in the ocean."

I sit back on my heels and study Evan's form.

"Oh, Evan, what am I going to do?" I mutter.

I'm checking his pulse again when he stops breathing. His chest shudders to a halt.

"No," I'm saying as I bend over him, "no, no, no, no, no."

I leap into action, my muscles working before my mind can catch up. I kneel over Evan, my hands pumping his chest. I pinch his nose, then bend and put my mouth to his.

It's like we're kissing.

The thought bounces through my mind. It's totally inappropriate. And it's not like I haven't kissed Evan before. Plus, this isn't kissing. This is to save his life.

Focus, India, I tell myself.

I breathe water into his lungs. I press his chest up and down with my hands. And I do all of this while tears are streaming down my cheeks.

"Wake up, Evan. Wake up!" I order.

More breaths. More pressing his chest.

Why did the storm have to take away my healing powers?

"Wake up. Please, Evan!" I'm begging now. "Why couldn't we be stuck in here with an electric eel and not some stupid jellyfish?" I demand. "At least I could have shocked your heart back to life."

The jellyfish blinks.

"Don't leave me in the darkness," I whisper, right before the light goes out.

Even in the darkness, I keep trying to save Evan. It's all I can do.

Then suddenly, a cough.

And another cough.

Evan's chest begins to rise and fall under my fingertips. His skin grows warmer. And he's coughing all over my lap.

The jellyfish flickers and weak light fills the cave. It's enough for me to see Evan's eyes open. He's breathing on his own, and his pulse is strong.

"India?" he asks. It's the most beautiful thing I've ever heard.

"Welcome back," I say.

Then I collapse in tears.

CHAPTER 10

"So I pushed you into the cave right before the rocks came down?" Evan asks.

"Yep, that's pretty much what happened," I say. This is the third time I've explained it.

"And I was out for a while," Evan says.

I nod, my hair rubbing against rock. After Evan woke up, I helped him get to the side of the cave. We're propped against the wall, across from the rock pile. Evan's tail stretches in front of him. Our arms are touching.

"It probably wasn't as long as it felt," I say.

"And you saved me," Evan says. I blush, hearing the note of wonder in his voice.

"I could have done better if I had my powers," I say.

"They're still gone?" he asks.

I flex my fingers. "Hm, let me try," I say.

I turn so I'm facing him. A tiny line of blood still trickles from his cut. I put my fingers over the bleeding and call up my powers.

After a moment, I drop my hand onto my leg.

"Nothing," I say.

Evan covers my hand with his. My insides light up at the touch. I'm so happy I almost miss hearing his words.

"What was that?" I ask.

"I said, your powers will return once the water settles," he says.

"That's what I hear," I say. "Once the oxygen levels go back to normal, mermaid powers will return."

"Soon, then," Evan says.

We sit in silence for a while. For the first time, I realize how quiet it is. I don't hear anything banging against the wall of the cave.

"Did the storm stop?" I ask.

"Maybe," Evan says. "It was noisier when I woke up. Although isn't there an eye of the storm? Isn't that the calm spot before it picks up again?"

"I suppose so," I say. "So more might be coming." My stomach sinks at the thought. But I'm relieved that Evan's okay.

Then I look at the pile of rocks blocking the entrance. They are too heavy for us to move ourselves. Our only hope is for the mer to reach us from the other side.

But what if no one finds us?

Evan tips his head against the wall. "What was the name you mentioned? When you got here?"

"Huh?" I ask. I'm distracted by Evan's fingers, which are tracing a pattern on my palm.

"You were saying something about a ... a sea witch? When you were talking to my dad and Ani?" Evan says.

"Oh, right," I say. "Morgan." I sit up and pull my hand away from Evan.

"Who's Morgan?" Evan asks.

"She lives in Grandpa's town. And she created the storm," I say. "Well, maybe not created it, but Grandpa thinks she made it stronger. And that she sent it to the mer."

"Why would anybody do that?" Evan sounds angry.

"I don't know," I say. "I know she hates the mer."

"But wait, the dance is miles from the canyons. How did she know to send it here?" Evan asks.

I shrug. Evan scoots away from me.

"Unless someone told her," he says.

I glare at him. "You think I told Morgan where the dance was?" I cry. "I would never do that. And I can't believe you think I would."

"Sorry," Evan mutters.

"Besides, the storm went right over the canyons," I point out.

"So maybe it's unlucky it hit the dance too," Evan comments.

"Yeah, right," I say. "The dance."

The words sound wooden when I speak. All I can picture is Evan swaying with Melody, her arms draped around his neck.

"You couldn't come to the dance," Evan says.

"No," I say.

"I asked," he offers.

I turn back to look at him. His face is in shadows. "You asked Melody to the dance? Yeah, I noticed."

Even in the darkness, I see Evan blush. "No. I mean yeah, I asked Melody to the dance. Well, she asked me, actually." He reaches for my hand again. His fingers are warm around mine. "But what I meant was that I asked Ani first."

I'm confused. "You asked Ani to the dance?"

Evan laughs, a low, warm sound. "No. My dad asked her first, anyway," he says.

"Really?" I say. "Wait, are they together?"

Evan shrugs. "Hard to tell. I think they went to the dance to set an example for the tribes. That we should all get along. But sometimes I think they like each other too."

"Wow, that's something," I say. "Kind of weird. Seeing your dad date." I shiver, thinking about my own parents. If they split up, they might date other people.

"Yeah," Evan says, squeezing my fingers.

"Where's your mum?" I ask. The words slip from my mouth.

Evan squirms and ducks his head. "She left," he says. "About a year ago."

"Where did she go?" I ask.

"A group of them left. They went to explore other canyons. In case we need to move again," he adds. "Lulu's dad is with the group too."

"Oh," I say. "Lulu never talks about her dad."

"It's hard not to feel like they picked the tribe over us," Evan says. "Maybe I shouldn't say that, but that's how I feel."

I nod, thinking about my own parents sending me away. I choke back tears and change the subject.

"Anyway, what did you ask Ani?" I say.

Evan pauses. When he speaks, his voice is a low murmur. "I asked her if you could come to the dance," he says.

The water catches in my throat. "You did?"

"Yeah, I did," he says.

"Why?" I ask. My voice is high and squeaky.

Evan leans forward. "India. You know why."

Then he leans further forward and puts his mouth against mine.

We've kissed a few times before. But never in a dark cave, all by ourselves. I twist so my arms are around his neck. One of his hands touches my hair.

I pull back to smile at him. Then I lean in to kiss him again.

But just as I do that, I hear rumbling outside.

"Oh, no," I say. I know what that sound means.

"Maybe it's someone coming to rescue us," Evan says, tilting his head to listen.

A rock slams against the outside of the cave, followed by two more. The rumbling gets louder, turning into a huge roar.

"I don't think that's the sound of rescue," I say. "The storm's back."

The wall we're leaning against shudders. Evan pushes away from the wall, pulling me with him.

"We need to get further into the cave," he says.

We swim as far back as possible, but the cave is shallow. The jellyfish follows us, hovering over our heads.

BAM!

Another rock hits the cave. Followed by another, and another.

"Hold on," Evan says. He pulls me into his arms, tucking my head under his. And we sit like this while the storm rages outside.

I lose track of time. I think I might sleep for a bit, which is weird since the storm is so loud. But I feel safe with Evan. I think he sleeps for a bit too. At one point the jellyfish goes out, and we sit in darkness.

I think about my friends. I hope they made it to safety. I don't let myself think about what happened if they didn't.

I can't help them now, I think. *I can only hope they're safe.*

At some point I drift off to sleep again. When I wake up, the storm is silent and faint light is trickling into the cave.

Evan is snoring softly against my shoulder.

"Hey, wake up," I say, nudging him.

He doesn't stir.

"Evan," I say, giving him a bigger shake. "Wake up." These are the same words I said to him earlier, when he was out cold. I'm relieved that all I need to do now is wake him from sleep.

Evan gives a snort and sits up. "Huh? What is it?" He rubs his eyes.

I take his hand and point. "Look," I say. There, at the top of the pile of rocks, is an opening.

"The storm must have knocked the rocks loose," Evan says.

He takes my hand, and we swim to the top of the rock pile. The opening is too narrow for either of us to swim through. But we can shout through it.

"Help! Help us!" we shout.

I can see glimpses of brighter waters and a few rocks. I can't see the bottom of the crater or any mer, however.

"We're up here!" I yell. "Help!"

Evan is breathing heavily next to me.

"Are you okay?" I ask.

"Fine," he says, clutching his ribs. "I'm just tired. You see anybody?"

"No one," I say, shaking my head. "You don't think they left us, do you?"

"I don't think so," Evan says. "Everyone probably hid in caves, just like we did."

"I hope so," I say. I don't share my deepest fears: *What if they're all dead?*

"Keep shouting," Evan says.

"Okay," I say. I turn back to the opening. "Help!" I yell. "Help!!"

"Whoa, whoa, whoa. No need to shout," a gruff voice replies.

A grey head pokes over the top of the rock pile. Bruce's face is streaked with grit. His eyes are red, as if he's been crying. But he's grinning at us.

"Bruce," I say, tears spilling down my face. "I've never been so happy to see anyone in my life."

"Let's get you out of here," he says.

CHAPTER 11

Bruce calls a few other mer over to our cave. I don't recognize any of them, but they start picking rocks off the pile blocking our entrance.

"The mermaids lost their powers after the storm," Bruce explains. "Otherwise we'd have one of them get you out of here fast."

"How is everyone?" Evan asks.

Bruce shrugs. "They're okay. Most of us took shelter in a nearby trench. We swam deep to avoid the worst of the waves."

"Is anyone hurt?" I ask.

"A few scrapes and cuts. Nothing worse than that," Bruce tells us. He keeps moving rocks as he talks.

"My dad?" Evan asks.

"He's fine," Bruce says. "I saw him earlier this morning."

"And my friends?" I ask, my voice shaking. "Lulu and Nari and Dana?"

"They're fine too," Bruce says. He's a man of few words.

"Can you tell them we're okay?" I ask.

Bruce glances over his shoulder and then back at us. He's grinning again. "You can tell them yourselves."

"India!" I can hear Lulu shouting. "India!" Her face appears in the opening, knocking Bruce aside. "You're okay!"

"And you're okay too!" I say, reaching for her.

We can't hug yet, because the opening isn't big enough. Instead we clutch each others' hands.

"India!" Dana bellows behind Lulu.

Lulu drops my hands, and Dana appears at the window. She is beaming. There's a scrape across her forehead.

"Are you okay?" I ask her.

"Oh, this?" she asks, pointing at her forehead. "I barely even notice it. How are you?" She catches sight of Evan, who waves. "Well, isn't this cozy?" Dana teases.

"My turn!" I hear Nari call. Dana disappears while Nari takes her place.

"India, we have so much to tell you!" she says.

"And you'll be able to tell her much faster if you all let us do our work," Bruce says.

"Oh, sure," Nari says. "Talk soon!"

"Wait," I say. "The storm. Do we know if it went to land or not?"

Bruce shakes his head. "Looks as if it came here and then went east. Don't think it went near shore."

"Thank goodness," I breathe. Grandpa should be safe.

"Now, let's get back to work," Bruce says. "These rocks aren't going to lift themselves."

The mer keep moving the rocks blocking our cave. Within ten minutes, they've moved enough for us to swim free.

Right before I leave the cave, Evan takes my hand, stopping me. "What?" I ask, confused.

He tugs me towards him gently. He rests his forehead against mine. "I just wanted to say thank you," he whispers. "For saving my life."

"Oh, it's ... it's no problem," I stammer.

"Ready, you two?" Bruce asks, interrupting the moment. He catches sight of us and winks. "Or should I give you another minute?"

Evan squeezes my hand and lets me go. "Let's get out of here," he says.

We swim free into a crowd of mer. I lose track of Evan. I can still feel the imprint of his hand around mine, though. Ani swims up to me.

"You darling girl," she says, giving me a hug. "You were very brave."

"Bruce said everyone's okay?" I ask.

"We are because of you," Ani says.

She starts speaking loudly. There are several dozen mer nearby. Heads start turning in her direction.

"We are safe because India Finch came to warn us," she calls in a loud awkward voice. "Your warning gave us enough time to get to the trenches. You risked your life to help us. Without you, we would have suffered great loss."

"Why are you doing this, Mum?" Lulu cries. "It's embarrassing."

"Look," Nari says, pointing at the crowd of mer. Most of them are nodding at me, and a few are smiling. Some of them are even fluttering their tails, as if they're clapping.

"Just wanted to make sure they know who to thank," Ani says.

Storm swims into view.

"India Finch," he growls.

"Storm," I reply.

He floats there for a long moment, just looking at me. He has a weird expression on his face, as if he has to fart or something.

"Did you have something to say, Storm?" Ani asks.

"I ... that is ... thank you for saving my son," he says. Then he swims away.

"Well, that's something, I suppose," I say. It was probably really hard for him to say anything halfway nice to me.

"Storm's coming around," Ani says. "He sees your worth to the mer."

"How did you save Evan?" Lulu demands. "Are your powers back?"

"No," I say. "I used first-aid training." My friends look at me blankly. "It's a human thing," I explain.

"Oh," they say.

"Come on," Ani says. "You can explain more on the way home."

"We're going back to the canyons?" I ask. "Now? You want to travel without your powers?"

"The ocean is dangerous to us either way," Ani explains. "Our powers won't return for a few days. We'd rather be on the move than stay here. And we want to see if there's any damage to the canyons. Storm and I both agree it's for the best."

At that moment, Storm gives a shout. "Let's go!" he calls. With that, all the mer follow Storm out of the crater.

As we make our way back to the canyons, my friends and I talk about our storm experiences.

"It was really scary," Nari says. "Ani told us all to get to the trench behind the crater. And the three of us got separated."

"Yeah, that was the worst," Dana says.

"So you all just swam to the bottom of this trench?" I ask.

Lulu nods. "The water was really cold," she says. "We swam as far down as we could. The storm passed us over."

"We all found each other once we got to the trench," Dana says.

"How long were you down there?" I ask.

"The entire time," Nari says. "It felt like forever."

"Tell me about it," I murmur.

My friends all laugh.

"We'd like to know more about what happened to you," Lulu says. "You were down in the cave the whole time?"

"With Evan?" Dana says with a grin.

"Nothing happened!" I protest. "Well, nothing much," I add. I can feel my face getting hot.

"Aha!" Lulu says. "I knew something happened! Tell us everything."

I glance around to make sure no one is listening to us. I notice Melody swimming ahead of us, glaring at us over her shoulder now and again.

I drop back so we have more privacy. "Um, well, we kissed," I say. My friends squeal.

"That's so great!" Dana says.

"But he almost died," I add.

My friends stare at me.

"Because you kissed?" Nari whispers.

Nari looks so serious, as if she really believes I might have killed Evan by kissing him. We all look at her, and then we all start laughing. Soon Nari is laughing too.

"No, he got hurt when the rocks fell," I explain. "I had to help him."

I could tell them more details. But I don't want to. Telling them about giving Evan CPR feels too private. It's something I only want to share with him.

"Do any of you have your powers back?" I ask. I want to change the subject.

Lulu raises her hands and tries to summon a current. "Nope," she says.

Dana moves her hands, trying to make the water thick. "I can't, either. Some of the older mer told me it usually takes a few days."

"We'll be back in the canyons in a few hours," Nari says. "Everything will be fine then."

"Let's just hope nothing bad happens between now and then," Lulu adds.

CHAPTER 12

We reach the canyons early that evening. My friends and I are near the back of the group. Word starts trickling back to us: the canyons are fine.

Dana swims ahead to see for herself. She's back in a few minutes.

"The storm came close to the canyons," she says, "so there are lots of rocks down. Some of the creatures got peeled off the sides of the canyons. But otherwise, things are fine."

"Good," Lulu says. "My mum will be relieved."

"And watch this," Nari says. She holds out her hand and wiggles her fingers. A lone sea horse bobs in Nari's direction.

"Wait, are you calling that sea horse?" Dana asks. "Or is she just wandering in this direction on her own?"

Nari gazes at the sea horse. "I can't say for certain," she admits.

"Here, let me try," Dana says. She flexes her hands. We wait for the water around us to turn thick.

After a moment, she drops her hands.

"Nothing," she says.

Lulu tries to summon a current of water, but nothing happens either. I don't even try to use my powers. I don't even want to scratch myself and not be able to fix it.

We reach the edge of the canyons. I see what Dana means about the damage. There are piles of rocks on the canyon floors. I mean, there are always rocks the canyon floor, but these are more than usual.

"Oh, no," Nari says, pointing at the side of a cliff. "That used to be covered in starfish. That was always my favourite."

Dana swims over to look.

"They'll come back, I'm sure," Dana says when she returns. She smiles at Nari.

"I hope so," Nari says.

Most of the mer are floating around the canyons, checking the damage. Daylight starts to fade.

"Um, can I stay with you guys?" I ask. "Assuming Ani doesn't send me home right away?"

"What about your grandpa?" Lulu asks.

"Oh, right. He's probably worried about me," I say. "But maybe I can stay for a little bit? Just to see how things are?"

Dana slings her arm around my shoulder. "Of course you can. Let's go and ask Ani."

We start swimming through the crowd looking for Ani. I'm also looking for Evan. I haven't seen him since we left the cave. He swam away with his dad at the front of the group. I don't mind. I needed some time to think about what happened.

I don't regret kissing Evan. But I still have to think about what it means. Evan can't live with me on land. And I'm not sure I want to live with the mer forever.

I'm lost in thought and run straight into Lulu.

"Ouch!" she says.

"Oh, sorry," I say, rubbing my shoulder. "You okay?"

"Yeah, fine," Lulu says. She sounds distracted. She's looking at a group of mer gathered near the entrance to Ice Canyon.

"What's going on?" I ask.

"I'm not sure," she says. "Something's happening, though."

The group of mer at the entrance look as if they're arguing about something. I catch sight of Ani in the middle of the group. She's pointing and shaking her head.

The four of us swim over to see what's going on.

"This has gone too far!" one mer is shouting. "Too many humans in the area." He shoots me a dirty look.

"We don't know what she wants," Ani says. She edges over to us. "Go back to your cave, girls. It's not safe here."

"What's happening?" I ask.

Ani shakes her head and glances at the surface of the water. "A boat is almost at the canyons. The guards report there are two people in it."

"Who are they?" Lulu asks.

"We're not sure," Ani says. "My guards are going to check it out further. Humans don't usually get this close to the canyons. Until we know more, I want you four to go to your cave."

"But–" Lulu says.

"Go," Ani interrupts. Her face softens. "You may not believe it, but it's for your own good."

"Fine," Lulu says. "We'll go."

"Wait, what's going to happen to the humans?" I ask.

Ani's eyes shift away from me. Is she about to lie to me?

"They will be taken care of," Ani says.

"How?" I ask.

Ani tries to turn away, but I swim in front of her.

"You're not going to hurt them," I say. "Right?"

Ani sighs. "We have to protect the canyons."

"So what does that mean?" I ask. "You'd hurt humans? Just like Storm would?"

"We'll try to end this without humans even knowing we're here," Ani says. "We will do everything we can not to hurt whoever's up there."

I hesitate.

"It's the best I can do, India," Ani says.

I square my shoulders and face the leader of Ice Canyon. "It's not good enough," I say.

Ani looks hurt by my words. "India–" she starts.

"Don't I mean anything to you?" I interrupt. "I'm part-human. But you're considering hurting the humans up there. You don't even know who they are or why they're here!"

There's a sound of someone clearing his throat nearby. We both turn to see Bruce approach.

"Well?" Ani asks.

Bruce's eyes flicker to me for a second. Dread fills me.

"There's a woman," Bruce says. "And a man. We don't know who the woman is."

Ani frowns. "And the man?"

Bruce looks at me again.

"It's Adam Finch," he says.

"Grandpa?" I gasp.

"Adam?" Ani asks. "Well, then. You'd better come with me, India."

We're silent as we make our way to the surface. I hear sounds of swimming behind me. I glance over my shoulder to see Lulu, Dana and Nari following us. Ani notices too.

"I can't keep the four of you apart, can I?" Ani murmurs.

Lulu looks over her shoulder. "You can't keep the rest of the mer from this, either."

A stream of mer are following us. I catch sight of Evan, followed by Storm. I see Melody's bright head near Evan. Behind them, dozens of Fire and Ice Canyon mer swim towards the surface. The boat bobs above us, tiny against the vast ocean.

Ani pauses right beneath the surface. "Ready?" she asks me.

I nod, and we break through the water.

It takes a few moments for everyone's lungs to adjust to breathing air. The sun dazzles our eyes. A cool breeze is blowing, which makes me shiver.

"You okay, India?" A gravelly, familiar voice reaches me.

I swim to the side of the boat and raise my hand. Grandpa reaches over and takes it.

"Hi, Grandpa," I say. I'm happy to see him.

"You survived the storm," he says.

"Yep. You too," I say.

"It went out to sea," he says. "We had rain, some wind. Could have been worse." He glances over his shoulder at the woman crouching in the front of the boat.

"Adam Finch," Ani says, swimming up behind me.

"Ani," he says, nodding his head.

"And you brought a friend," she comments.

Grandpa shakes his head. "Not a friend. Morgan said she'd send another super storm if I didn't take her to you."

"You are behind the storm?" Ani asks, addressing Morgan.

The sea witch stirs. She turns her head slowly to look at Ani.

"And I will send another one. Worse than this. One that will destroy all of your homes," Morgan says.

"But how can that be?" Grandpa says softly. "You didn't send the first one."

Morgan glares at him. "I may not have created the storm, but I controlled it once it got close enough. I made it strong. I sent it towards the mer."

Ani holds on to the side of the boat. "Why?" she asks.

Morgan leans over the side. The boat sways.

"Because the mer do not deserve to live!" she spits.

Ani draws a deep breath. She keeps her voice calm. "Those are harsh words," she says. "What have we ever done to anger you?"

"You know who I am," Morgan says.

"We haven't met," Ani says. "But I know who you are. You are Morgan, a sea witch. I have heard stories about you."

"I expected that you would," Morgan boasts.

"I know you knew Jamal," Ani says. She nods at Grandpa. "Adam's son." Then Ani nods at me. "India's father."

Morgan smirks at me. "Hello, India," she says, waving her fingers. I glare at her.

Ani clears her throat, and Morgan looks back at her. "I also know that you hate the mer," Ani says.

"Because of what you did to Jamal," Morgan spits. "You ruined him."

Grandpa shakes his head. "Jamal was at fault too."

"You don't know that," Morgan says. She glares at Grandpa. "He never told you what happened. How that mermaid died."

Around me, all of the mer freeze.

"Did he tell you?" Ani whispers.

Grandpa and I don't know exactly what happened years ago. My dad refuses to talk about it. I asked him once, and he clammed up. Ani knows some details but not the whole story. Is Morgan going to fill in the blanks for us?

Morgan's shoulders drop. "He never told me. I suppose he didn't trust me enough." She shoots me another angry look. "Instead he left and started a new life."

"So why come here now?" Ani asks. "Why send the super storm?"

Morgan raises her head. Is it my imagination, or did the wind just rise too?

"You are the reason Jamal left. All of you. And you deserve to die," Morgan hisses.

"Morgan–" Grandpa starts to say.

The sea witch cuts him off with a wave of her hand. "Quiet," she says.

The wind picks up. The waters start to churn. I bounce against the boat.

"What's she doing?" someone asks.

"Morgan, stop this," Ani demands.

"No," Morgan says. "I will not stop this. And I know that you can't stop it, either. The storm took away your powers."

She stands up in the boat, raising her hands. The wind gets stronger. Lightning flickers in the sky, making all of the mer flinch.

Grandpa lurches towards Morgan. I think he's going to push her out of the boat. At the last minute, she whips her hand towards him. A small blast of lightning hits him in the chest. He falls backwards into the bottom of the boat.

"Grandpa!" I shriek. I swim towards the boat.

A wave comes out of nowhere. I cry in anger as the water carries me away from the boat.

Ani shouts, "Morgan, stop!"

Morgan laughs. The eerie sound stretches over the water.

"I cannot be stopped," she says. "And you cannot do anything to stop me. You don't have your powers. The storm was only the beginning."

With that, Morgan screams at the top of her lungs. It's not words, just a horrible sound.

For a moment, there is silence.

And then a monster emerges out of the deep.

CHAPTER 13

"No!" Nari screams right into my ear.

A swirling mass of tentacles breaks the surface of the water. It's followed by a long, pointed beak and a single, horrible eye.

I'm frozen as I stare at it. "What is it?" I shout.

My answer comes in the shouts and screams of the mer.

"It's a squid!" someone shouts. "Giant squid!"

We are in horrible danger. Aside from sharks, giant squids are the only sea creatures that prey on mer.

"Oh, no," Lulu whispers. "We have to get out of here now!"

"I'm not going to be dinner!" Dana says. She grabs my hand, and the four of us swim.

The mer are swimming everywhere, trying to get out of the path of the squid. It's like trying to get across the dance floor. I get elbowed in the ribs. Tail fins scratch my legs. And I can't see where we're going.

Dana's hand gets ripped from mine. All I can hear is shouting.

"Where are you?" I scream. My voice is lost in the clamour.

I've lost all sense of direction. I have no idea if I'm swimming away from the squid or straight towards it. I'm knocked from behind. I swallow a mouthful of water. Arms and tails churn past me.

I'm bumped again and am pushed underwater. I stay below and try to swim to safety. There are dozens of mer here, their eyes wide with terror. I scan their faces for my friends but don't see them.

I see an open patch of water and swim towards it. I'm pretty sure I'm still heading away from the squid. I need to get to the boat. I need to make sure Grandpa is okay. I don't know what I'd do if he wasn't.

The water is lighter up ahead. I push towards it, eventually surfacing.

And I come face-to-face with the giant squid.

It flails on the surface of the water, tentacles waving everywhere. The tentacles part to reveal a horrible beak. Two sharp pincers are opening and closing, just waiting to eat something. Just waiting to eat me.

"Oh, no," I whisper.

The squid is between the boat and me. I glance over my shoulder. Behind me, there is open water. And the mer.

The mer have stopped swimming. Everyone is staring at the squid. Staring at me. We're all motionless, except for the squid. It is coming straight towards us.

"India!" I hear Lulu shout.

Over the teeming mass of the squid, I can see Morgan standing in the boat.

"Attack!" she shouts.

The squid comes towards us. It's a horrifying sight. Tentacles reach out, slapping the water. The beak snaps open and closed, looking for something to eat.

I'm frozen in the water. I wonder if this is it. Is this the end of me? Funny, I never thought I'd die by being eaten by a giant squid. I imagine my friends in Birmingham hearing the news. They'd be sad, but they might also laugh a little. And I wouldn't blame them. Who gets killed by a giant squid? It's stupid.

"Nope, not going to happen to this girl," I mutter to the squid. Then I dive deep underwater.

I surface fifty feet away. I'm further from the boat, but this is part of my plan.

"Hey!" I shout, swimming towards the squid. I'm waving my hands. "Hey!"

The squid pauses for a second. Its huge eye rolls towards me. It's disgusting.

"Over here!" I yell.

The squid turns and starts heading my way. I can see the mer glancing at each other, wondering what I'm doing.

"Confuse it!" I shout to them. The squid keeps swimming towards me.

Lulu emerges from the crowd. "India, are you crazy?" she shouts.

The squid halts at the sound of her voice. Then it starts swimming towards Lulu.

Understanding dawns on Lulu's face. "India's right!" she says. "We have to confuse it. Spread out."

Lulu swims to the right. Dana and Nari shoot out of the crowd and start swimming towards me.

"Come on! Help us!" Lulu shouts to the other mer.

The mer slide into action, fanning out to surround the squid. They start shouting and splashing. The squid doesn't know which way to turn. It lunges towards one group of mer, who swim out of the way.

Another group of mer starts yelling, and the squid changes direction. Some of the mer must have dived for rocks, because they are tossing stones at the squid.

This makes the squid even angrier.

I can hear Morgan shouting. "Attack them! Attack!"

The squid thrashes harder. Its tentacles seem to grow longer. It turns, looking for a victim.

And finds Evan.

"No!" I shriek.

Evan is swimming off to the side, all alone. The squid moves towards him, its beak gaping.

"Evan!" I yell.

All of the mer are watching, but no one is close enough to help. It's up to me. I have to save Evan.

I dive below the surface of the water, swimming as fast as I can. I see Evan's green tail. Behind him is the squid.

I grab Evan's tail fin and pull him under.

He sputters, surprised.

"Swim!" I shout. "Get out of here!"

Behind us, the squid has also ducked beneath the surface of the water. It's coming towards us.

"Go!" I shout.

Evan looks stunned. A tentacle snakes towards us. The sight snaps Evan from his daze.

"No!" he cries.

"Let's go!" I shout. I take his hand and pull him after me. We swim as fast as we can. I can see the rest of the mer in front of us. Most have come below the surface of the water.

Oh, no! We're leading the squid right towards the mer, I realize.

I let go of Evan's hand. "Go!" I yell. "You have to keep confusing it! Get the others to help."

Evan looks confused. "What about you?"

"I'll be fine," I say. I swim away before he can protest.

Water churns around me. I can barely see. But I swim as fast as I can. I need to get to the boat.

There, I think. I spot the boat hovering on the surface above me.

I swim as fast as I can until I'm above the water. I gasp as my lungs adjust to air. My eyes squint in the sunlight. The boat is right in front of me.

Morgan has her back to me, her arms raised. I hook my hands on the boat and pull myself up. I'm afraid of what I might see in the bottom of the boat.

Grandpa lies with his eyes closed. His arms are flung open. He's not moving.

"Grandpa?" I squeak. Tears are running down my face. I almost lost Evan. I'm not going to lose Grandpa.

Very carefully I pull myself over the side of the boat. Morgan is so busy controlling the squid that she doesn't notice. I crouch near the back of the boat.

"Grandpa?" I whisper. My shadow falls across his face. And his eyes crack open.

"India?" he asks.

I scoot forwards, wiping tears from my face. "Hi, Grandpa."

He raises his head and sees Morgan.

"She's still causing problems," he says.

"We have to stop her," I say.

Grandpa nods and sits up.

"Are you hurt?" I whisper.

"A little achy," he says. "But that could just be because I'm old."

I help Grandpa to his feet. The motion makes the boat rock. Morgan turns around, her arms falling.

"End it," Grandpa says before she can speak.

"You aren't strong enough to stop me," she says.

"End it," Grandpa repeats.

"No," she says.

"If you're angry at my dad, don't take it out on the mer," I say. "Send the squid away."

Morgan's face goes white. "Your father broke my heart. He chose that silly mermaid over me. But he won't get away with it. I will have my revenge!" she cries.

"Morgan–" Grandpa begins, but his words get cut off as the boat begins to shake.

"What's happening?" I ask.

Morgan laughs, a terrible, raw sound. "I'm getting my revenge," she says as the boat shakes harder.

Tentacles wrap around the sides of the boat.

"Oh, no," I whisper, clinging to Grandpa's arm. The giant squid is underneath the boat.

"If the squid crushes the boat, it will crush you too," Grandpa says to Morgan. "India and I can survive in the water. But you will die."

"Not if the squid eats you first," Morgan says. She sneers at us. "You will lose everything, Adam Finch. And so will they."

She gestures to the mer, who are watching from afar. I can see my friends staring at us. I can see their fear from here.

"Stop this, Morgan!" Grandpa shouts. The boat starts to crack as the tentacles tighten.

"Never!" Morgan yells. The bottom of the boat splits. Water starts pouring in. I try to stay calm, but I'm clinging to Grandpa.

"You will not take my granddaughter from me. I will never let that happen!" he cries.

I'm not sure who moves first. Grandpa or Morgan? Or me?

The three of us meet in the middle of the boat. Morgan grabs my arms. She is pushing and pulling, tugging me towards the side.

"Say goodbye, little girl," she hisses in my ear. A tentacle wraps itself around my wrist and starts to tug.

"India!" Grandpa shouts. He's behind Morgan, pulling at her shoulders. I lash out with my foot. I hit Morgan's shin. She winces and drops my arm. I'm almost free.

But then the squid tugs, and I start to go over.

"No!" Grandpa shouts.

Everything becomes very blurry. Grandpa's face looms in front of mine, his eyes wide. He reaches for me. Our fingers brush. Then Morgan is in front of me. Her hands are on my arms. The three of us are struggling. The squid pulls at me. I'm almost in the water.

I kick my feet. I hit something. Morgan slumps and her fingers loosen. In that split second, the boat tips.

Grandpa grabs my wrist and pulls me free. And Morgan falls over the side of the boat, into the tentacles of the giant squid.

The tentacles catch her and drag her under. The squid disappears. Grandpa and I are left in the sinking boat, staring at the spot where Morgan disappeared beneath the waves.

CHAPTER 14

"So she's really gone? We're sure she's gone?" I ask for the hundredth time.

"She's gone," Ani says, handing me a bunch of seaweed. I nibble mindlessly on the snack.

"Our guards tracked the squid for miles," Storm says. "She was with it. It turned into deeper water, heading south. We stopped following."

The seaweed catches in my throat. I cough to clear it, not wanting to ask the next question. "Was she ... was she dead?"

Storm shrugs his massive shoulders. "We could not tell. But she does not have mer heritage. She is a sea witch, though. Perhaps her magic allows her to breathe underwater."

"Maybe," I say.

But I can't get the final image of Morgan out of my head. She fell into the tentacles of the monster. I can't shake the feeling that she fell to her death. And that Grandpa and I helped her.

Storm peers at me. "Why does it matter, India Finch? She was your enemy. Why do you care if she still lives?"

"Because she's a person," I say. The answer blurts out. "She was terrible, but that doesn't mean I want her dead."

Storm watches me. Grandpa lays his hand on my shoulder and gives it a squeeze.

"We did what we had to do, India," Grandpa says. "You didn't try to kill her. Neither did I."

"I kicked her," I blurted. "And she lost her balance and fell. It's my fault."

Grandpa shakes his head. "You kicked her, and I shoved her shoulder. It was the same moment when the boat tipped. Those actions caused her to fall."

"*We* caused her to fall," I protest.

"Yes, we were a part of it," Grandpa says. "But don't forget, Morgan is to blame too. She summoned the squid. And she wanted to hurt you. I wasn't going to let that happen."

I nod and squeeze Grandpa's hand. I know he's right. But I also know I'll never forget the sight of Morgan disappearing beneath the waves.

Storm is still watching us. "You're a strange girl," he says at last. "But you did save my son's life."

"Twice," I say.

Storm laughs, a deep, surprisingly nice sound.

"Twice," he confirms. He glances at Evan, who sits on my other side. When we got to Ani's cave after Morgan disappeared, Evan swam right over to sit next to me. He glared at his dad, daring Storm to make him move.

To our surprise, Storm didn't seem to care. Maybe me saving Evan – twice – has finally made Storm respect me. At least a little.

It occurs to me that the cave is full of the people I love. Lulu, Dana and Nari. My grandfather. Ani. Evan. Even though the thought of loving Evan makes me blush.

"So ... can India stay for a little while, Mum?" Lulu asks.

"We didn't summon her," Ani says. Her words make my heart droop. "But she did save us by warning us about the storm."

"And she put herself in danger," Storm interrupts. "She placed herself between the mer and the squid. India saved Evan." He turns his eyes on me. "That shows true bravery."

"India has always been brave," Grandpa says.

I'm starting to blush under all this attention.

"So that settles it?" Lulu asks. "India can stay?"

Ani's laugh sounds tired. "Will there ever be a time when you're not asking me if India can stay?"

"Yes, once she decides to live here with us," Lulu says. She nudges me with her elbow.

All eyes turn towards me. My blush deepens.

"We just survived a super storm and a squid," Grandpa says, answering for me. "Let's not worry about the future right now."

"Good point," Ani says. "For now, the Finches will be our guests."

"For how long?" Lulu presses.

Ani opens her mouth, but it's Storm who answers. "For as long as they like," he says.

He raises his handful of seaweed as if he's toasting me. I return the gesture, even though it feels awkward.

Ani claps her hands. "Let's celebrate! More seaweed for everyone."

With that, we sit together in the cave, laughing and telling stories. I get to spend time with my friends and with Evan. Grandpa is here, and I feel like a part of my heart is complete. We're all together.

It might not be forever. It might not even last through tomorrow. Morgan might be dead. Or she might be out there somewhere, plotting her next move against us. But for now, we are together, and that's all that matters.

ABOUT THE AUTHOR

Although **Julie Gilbert's** masterpiece, *The Adventures of Kitty Bob: Alien Warlord Cat,* has sadly been out of print since Julie last stapled it together in the fourth grade, she continues to write. Her short fiction, which has appeared in numerous publications, explores topics ranging from airport security lines to adoption to antique wreaths made of hair. Julie makes her home in southern Minnesota, USA, with her husband and two children.

ABOUT THE ILLUSTRATOR

Kirbi Fagan is a vintage-inspired artist living in the Detroit, Michigan, area, USA. She is an award-winning illustrator who specializes in creating art for young readers. She received her bachelor's degree in illustration from Kendall College of Art and Design. Kirbi lives by two words: "Spread joy". She is known to say, "I'm in it with my whole heart". When not illustrating, Kirbi enjoys writing stories, spending time with her family and rollerblading with her dog, Sophie.

GLOSSARY

clamour a loud and confused noise

clutch to hold on to something tightly

crater the mouth of a volcano or geyser

deafening very loud, as in a deafening crash

extinction the state of having died out

gesture an action that shows a feeling

glaring to look at someone in a very angry way

hover to stay attentively near by

loom to appear in a sudden or frightening way

lurch to move in an unsteady, jerky way

steamer ship a boat powered by steam

therapy a treatment for an illness, an injury or a disability, as in art therapy or speech therapy

FURTHER DISCOVERIES

1. India is an outsider to the mer world, even though she is half-mermaid. How does she handle this? Do you think she handles it well?

2. This story is told by India. What if the story was told from Morgan's point of view? How would the story be different?

3. Explain why India was so upset to learn about the dance. Have you ever experienced something similar?

4. What is the climax of the story? What makes it the climax?

5. Discuss India's character traits. What do we know about India based on her actions in this book? Does she remind you of anyone you know or any characters from other books or films?

WRITING INSPIRATION

1. All of India's mer friends look different. Write about how you would look if you were a mermaid. What colour would your tail be? Would you have a special power?

2. Explain why India feels like an outsider in the ocean, despite being part-mer. Compare this to her life on land.

3. Imagine that the day has come when India is ready to decide to either remain on land full time or live with the mer in the ocean. Which life does India choose? Write a scene that shows India sharing her choice with someone she loves.

4. In this story, there are two different tribes. Make up your own mer tribe. What is it called? What type of environment do they live in? How do they feel about humans?